The Reconstruction Of Cassiopeia

Leon Michaels

This is a work of Fiction. Any similarities to individuals past or present is unintentional and purely a coincidence. Any similarities to any individual in the future is pure Karma.

Acknowledgements

To my wonderful wife of over Forty-Seven years who tolerates my isolation while writing, the tolerates my begging her to read what I tried to write, then who puts up with my insane explanations of why I wrote what I wrote.

She deserves better……..!

And to the Ancient Greeks who gave us such a beautiful name…. Cassiopeia.

Also my thanks to those who risk reading this. I do hope it is entertaining.

Books by Leon Michaels
Stand Alone Action/Adventure

The Path Home

From the Mists of Darkness

Task Force Nemesis

Tales From The Bench

The Echelon Factor

Today is Yesterday's Tomorrow

Stand Alone ScFi

The Morbius Expedition

Random Acts Of Science Fiction

A Rigged Deck

Willem

A Lancer's Tale

Soraya

The Reconstruction of Cassiopeia

Post- Apocalyptic

Three Against The Darkness

"The Crane Equation Trilogy"

The Crane Equation: The Early Years

The Crane Equation: Rebuilding a Nation

The Crane Equation: The Crane Legacy

Action/Adventure

"The Black Ops Series"

Operation Damocles

Operation Dokkaebi

Operation Yofune-Nushi

Operation Kartikeya

The Black Orchid

The Twenty-First Special Operations Group: Book One: Family

The Twenty-First Special Operations Group: Book Two: Operators

Operation Heracles

Operation Pandora

Operation Pegasus

ScFi-Action/Adventure

"The Denoyelles Family Saga"

The Hanover Throne

The Bellus Project

The Bellus Legacy

The Bellus Myth

The Bellus Solution

The Bellus Prophecy

The Phoenix Project

The Bellus Curse

The Halfling

This Page Left Blank

The Back Story

The history of Constructs, humans built in a laboratory by blending technology and Biology, goes back to the Twentieth Century Terra, then known as Earth. It started in the minds of writers of what was called Comic Books, or later referred to as Graphic Novels.

The people so enhanced were heroes, male and female, who fought using their special strengths and powers to defeat evil in each story, or story arc over several of those books. In the early part of the Twenty-First Century, many of those characters made their way onto video for the entertainment of all viewers of all ages.

But these heroes were Cyborgs, part machine, part human.

It was in the Twenty-Eighth Century, as mankind was beginning to explore the stars, attempts were made to develop androids to assist in their travels. Androids could survive the decades travel between worlds, navigating the ships and caring for their cargo of hibernating humans without the need for food or water.

This met with limited success, but ultimately ended in the Android Revolt of 3133 A.D.. It would later be determined that the Revolt was caused by a computer virus introduced into the central Terrain Computer which sent upgrades to the Androids. The human programmer who wrote and introduced the virus into the Androids programming, was hung, shot, then quartered. His remains were cremated, then shot into Earth's Sun.

It would not be until the Thirty-Ninth Century that a real break-through would occur in the field of Bio-Mechanics and it would take a Bio-Physicist to accomplish that. Grahame Smuthers built on a rumor that there had been a successful Construct made in the Thirty-Fifth Century at John Hopkins on Terra, but the lab was destroyed in a fire and it is said the Construct, rumored to be known as Zaria, was also destroyed in that fire along with her creator.

Professor Smuthers as he was commonly known, worked with nanites, specifically what was commonly known as the Lazarus Tank. It was during the restructuring of an industrialist, injured in a space car race, that he came upon the idea of reprogramming the nanites in a more detailed way. Program them to construct as much as reconstruct.

But as a specialist in this field, he knew that in the current configuration, the nanites actually only repaired an injured subject within limitations. Some victims were too badly damaged to be, in the words of those familiar with the process, tanked. Smuthers felt this could be taken even further, and instead of constructing a body, reconstructing one as it was being repaired.

Smuthers spent five years researching the archives of John Hopkins via the Space Inter-link until he came upon the proposal of a Doctor Amos Jefferson to utilize the Lazarus Tank to correct fatal birth defects. Further research only told Smuthers that Jefferson had gained sponsors, primarily wealthy parents whose children were so inflicted. Jefferson had also died in the fire that destroyed his lab, along with his entire research staff.

All notes, all research into Jefferson's eight years of research were destroyed in the fire. This sent Smuthers into overdrive as he dissected Jefferson's proposal. Jefferson's proposal was to remove the living brain of the inflicted child, implant a micro-computer, ten percent larger than a sugar cube into the brain, then set the brain into a super-light, super alloyed skeleton before using purified DNA from the child to construct a normal human body around the frame.

Smuthers ran a dozen simulations on the concept and determined that it was possible to achieve a stable human form in this manner. But Smuthers took it one step closer to a natural body in further simulations by placing the entire body into a tank, then programming the nanites to repair and reconstruct the defective body while removing the defects. The results would not be in creating a Cyborg, but an enhanced human being with abilities similar to a Cyborg, but still, a human being, with human emotions, and dreams.

8

Also the nanites had the capability of forming a micro-computer within the brain without exposing it to the hazards of removing it from its host. Jefferson had made a notation to his proposal that nanites be embedded within the hosts body to keep said body under repair, and controlled by the micro-computer within the brain.

At first glance this seemed plausible, but as Smuthers worked the problem deeper, he came to the conclusion that unless there was a code within the computer allowing free will of the host, it could take over all actions and functions of the host. It could take away the free will of the host, without regard to the circumstances in which the host was functioning.

Then there was the question whether or not the micro-computer could be acted upon by an outside computer, taking over the host and using it for nefarious deeds. This is where the initial coding of the nanites would be important.

Smuthers recognized that one line of programing, one part of code being corrupted could cause the entire program to come crashing down, destroying a human life in the process, even once out amongst humanity.

One other function of the micro-computer which did not appear in Jefferson's proposal was that being linked to the human brain, the computer could be a store house of knowledge which might take decades for the host to accumulate normally.

Smuthers would spend three years utilizing a five liter tank to program its nanites then utilizing a small dog, that had been injured and facing euthanasia, tested his base theory. It would take nearly six months before the animal was withdrawn from the tank, whole and gentle to all those who it came into contact with.

Smuthers had his proof of concept. Now he needed funding and a subject to put through the process. Funding came from an unusual source, one he did not apply too. It came from the Planetary Marshalls Service via their Customs and Commerce Division.

9

The Marshalls also provided him with a test subject in the body of a Marshall who had been so badly injured that he was in a vegetation state and not eligible to be placed in a standard Tank for repairs and return to duty.

He was missing his right arm below the elbow and both legs below the knees. The damage to his torso required mechanical assistance to breath and process nutrients to keep him alive. His head was crushed, deformed, with one eye socket empty due to the injury.

Smuthers advised the Marshalls Service the process to repair this individual could take two or more years. The Service told Smuthers to do what had to be done and if successful, it would be worth the cost.

A three hundred and fifty liter tank was purchased and filled with virgin nanites. Once the tank came up to temperature and the computer link to the tank proved stable, the subject was placed in the tank under the watchful eyes of two Marshalls.

It would take twenty-seven months to repair and rebuild the subject which Smuthers only knew as Patient X.

Twenty-four hours before Patient X was removed from the tank, his entire bio-physical was completed showing he was functioning as normal as any human who had never been injured. His eyesight was near perfect with a new eye to replace the one destroyed in the incident as it was described to Smuthers. His head was reformed to match what is was prior to the incident and all biological functions were with human norm.

His missing limbs had been repaired and covered with muscle and flesh. Every perimeter required was covered, especially his brain functions. The only question the Marshalls had at this point was if Patient X could recall the moments prior to his injuries. All Smuthers could comment on was unless those brain cells were damaged or destroyed, he should retain all memories up to the point of becoming vegetative.

Medics from the Marshalls Service were brought in to assist in the removal of Patient X, then while still semi-conscious, he was taken away under heavy guard.

This left Smuthers only the computer data in which to write his paper to submit to the Hawkings Institute for Higher Learning.

Forty-eight hours later, Smuthers was once again visited by the Marshalls advising him that all data, all information concerning his research and the rehabilitation of Patient X was now classified as Top Secret, and he would not be able to submit his paper in hopes of receiving the Hawkings Trophy for Bio-Mechanics.

What did happen was Smuthers was taken along with his three lab assistants, and their families to Alpha Centuri Three, commonly known as Magnus, and placed in a laboratory ten times the size of the one he had been working in, and given almost a blank check to continue his research.

A month after arrival at his new labs, Smuthers met with Patient X who thanked him for his research and help returning him back into a functioning human being. Smuthers would later learn that Patient X had memories of where evidence was hidden which put away four Senators of the Planetary Parliament for Custom's violations, and attempted murder of a Customs Agent, who was Patient X. Included in those charges were the murders of two other Customs Agents who did not survive the attack on them.

Smuthers next patient was an eleven year old girl born with several birth defects, and whose life was nearing its end. Her limbs were deformed and her internal organs were shutting down when she was placed in the five hundred liter tank which had been provided at Smuthers new lab.

One specification was included in her treatment that required additional programming and that was once she was removed from the tank, her mind and body would be that of a twenty year old, in top physical condition.

Her name was Cassiopeia. And this is her story and the risk of merging Artificial Intelligence with a human in such a manner.

The Process

There was nothing simple about processing an individual through the tanking process. When looking at a tank without a client, it looked like it was full of a thick, silvery fluid. Once the client was introduced, the fluid looked alive, constantly moving in random patterns.

The introduction of the client was the moment of greatest risk as it was computed that three percent of the clients would reject basically being drowned in the fluid environment of the tank. The highest priority of each nanite was to provide oxygen to the client once submerged in the matrix.

Once the computers determined that the client was stable, nanites worked their way into the brain and formed the initial micro-computer, then began linking to the neural connections of the brain.

Again, once this procedure was complete, the nanites began providing nutrients to the body and removed all waste. No other procedure would begin until the client was stable with all neural links established.

When it was determined that client was stable, the DNA of the client was examined, and any defective genes were repaired or removed. This provided a stable base within the client to begin the rebuilding process.

It was during this time for Cassiopeia that the Marshalls brought in five more tanks, computers and five more subjects, four males and one female, all near the end of their time due to birth defects.

In addition to the tanks, the newest super-computer available was brought in, and all of the tanks computers were tied to it with a staff of Marshalls specifically trained in computer technology. There would be at least two Marshalls watching the now primary computer at all times.

When Smuthers needed to make and input to any tanks program, it was done at the master computer by a Marshall, and simulations were ran before the new code was downloaded.

The physical standards for serving in the Marshalls Service was set aside for this project. A female joining the Service had to be at a minimum of one point six meters tall. This provided the mass to height necessary to preform many of their duties. But with the enhanced strength predicted with this project, the females could be as small as one point four meters tall.

Each subject had been scanned into the computers and their childhood appearance was altered inside the computer until the desired result, appearance was determined, then it was fed to the nanites to do the reconstruction as they also repaired the subjects DNA and medical problems. The physical adjustments in the bodies only came once the medical problems had been eliminated.

There was no set time frame for each step, each process, as each body had separate problems to be dealt with in the time it took to correct those problems.

Within a month of the last subject clearing the last hurdle, the children started school.

This was a unique situation as it was determined that for one, they needed an education, one that their illnesses had prevented. Also, even though they were connected by the master computer, they could interact as normal children in constructed scenarios which they could act upon and react too. In their minds, what they experienced was as real as if they were normal children in a normal school environment.

Psychologists for the Marshalls Service determined that for the subject to be able to interact with those they came in contact with once the process to repair their bodies was completed, they had to experience as normal a childhood as possible. Their parents and teachers during the process were actually holographic copies of their actual parents, and both male and female Marshalls standing in as teachers. Actions and reactions for the adults came from the base computer program.

14

Cassiopeia quickly became friends with the other female, Mala, a dark skinned girl her same age. The boys were named Jefferson, Simon, Robert, and Gunther.

Once the rebuilding process was started on all of the children, the computer computed the time needed for each child to the date of completion of the reconstruction process. Robert would take longest of all of them with Jefferson completing the process first. Cassiopeia would be the third to complete the process if estimates were correct.

Interactions

The computer maintained a strict schedule for the subjects as far as day and night was concerned in preparation for the day they would be released to the real world. Each had their own rooms and interaction between their computer generated parents and teachers were important to their psychological growth.

Birthdays were celebrated with parties held at the individuals computer generated home as it was important each subject would grow out of the tanks with pleasant memories of childhood.

Their education was handled in such a manner that even though they interacted in a daily classroom, much of the information they received was via information input through their micro-computers.

The concept of exercise within the games the children played seemed unwarranted except their bodies reacted in the tanks as if they were actually doing the exercise, toning the muscles that were being repaired or replaced in their damaged bodies.

By the time the average age of the subjects was fourteen, they moved from their homes to dorm rooms as they started a university education schedule. This put in place a different set of rules concerning interaction between males and females.

Professor Smuthers found he had very little to do except stand back and observe what was happening to the subjects. When he looked at the schedule of interaction between the subjects outside of the classroom, he protested as the subjects were mere children to him.

The lead Psychologist informed Smuthers that interaction between the sexes at the age of fourteen was not uncommon as most people believed, and that their futures depended on being comfortable with those of the opposite sex, or even same sex.

Decades of study by Fleet Psych Docs on the treatment and recovery of personnel by the Lazarus process showed when possible, interaction while in the comatose state with computer generated images of loved ones, friends, or even strangers played a vital part in their recovery.

In the case of Cassiopeia and her group, their lives had been one of loneliness, isolation during the years they lived before being introduced to the tanks. It was vital they interact as much as possible with their peers, in their new shapes, to adjust their minds to what they would encounter once they were free of the process and out in society.

The problem that existed with the subjects being isolated in their tanks was actual, physical contact. This was resolved with the nanites applying pressure, or the sensation of touch during casual contact, but what of the feelings that go with something like a simple kiss?

The Marshalls Service took the work of the Fleet one step further in that they were able to read a couples physical reactions and emotions through sensors attached to their bodies during interaction. This allowed the computers to feed those emotions, feelings to the subjects involved, female to female and male to male, during interaction. Smuthers was aware of the interaction of kissing, but was not aware that the Marshalls studies went all the way to intercourse.

Interaction of a physical nature first took place at a party in the dorms playing an old Terran game called Spin The Bottle. Cassiopeia spun her bottle and it pointed towards Robert. They went out into the hallway and shared their first kiss, with the computer keeping time with their movements insuring the feelings stored in the main frame flowed into the subjects.

Before the night was over, Cassiopeia had kissed each boy and even Mala. This led to such interaction between the sexes over the next weeks, and the computer provided the stimulation and feelings when hands touched specific areas of the body and lips touched lips.

Other than kissing and light petting, none of the subjects interacted beyond that point until one night, Mala entered

17

Cassiopeia's room and after a short conversation, ended up on Cassiopeia's bed engaged in sexual activity. Again, the knowledge of performing such activity was supplied via the micro-computers, and the pleasure both girls felt was supplied by the main frame computer.

It was determined that the programing of free will into the subjects personality was the force behind Mala's attention to Cassiopeia. The artificial voices given to each subject gave the Psychologists volumes of data concerning how the program was progressing as far as their mental condition was at this point.

A week later, Mala took Gunther to bed, only performing oral sex on him as he returned the favor. Cassiopeia took Jefferson to bed two nights later after talking with Mala about the experience. But they were not the only ones engaging in such activity as the boys also began to interact in such a way.

One of the female Psychologist determined that even though they had programs for intercourse between the subjects, they did not have one for the removal of a virgin's hymen. Even though intercourse between the subjects in this state would ignore that the females had their hymens and were physical virgins, once removed from the tanks, this could cause confusion, even distress if not properly dealt with.

The subjects programs were put on hold while programing of the nanites took place to gently remove the females hymens.

This part of the process, the sexual interactions of the subjects was classified and only the Psychologists involved in the program could review the video of the subjects actions in the tanks, the holographic video of the actual interaction, and the Biological data stream during, and after the event.

On Cassiopeia's sixteenth birthday, she entertained all four boys and Mala in an orgy that lasted all night. Mala did the same on her sixteenth birthday. The Psychologists were near termination of this part of the program as they felt they were helping to create females with no inhibitions for physical contact once they were out of the tanks. But conversations between Mala

18

and Cassiopeia gave them reason to continue the program as both agreed it was fun, but not something to continue with.

When one of the boys suggest a party on his birthday, the girls agreed, but left the other boys out. During the rest of the program, there was never another mass sexual party between the subjects.

Since the subjects were in a university setting, the computer was able to generate over a thousand 'students and teachers' to fill in the background and even interact with in a social setting. When one of the subjects interacted further than just students, once again the computer generated the feelings and emotions required during such activity, but no two sets or acts ever felt the same, much like real life.

Smuthers had basically been shut out of the programs except to insure the base process was performing properly, but he discovered the sexual content of the process and became upset, loudly voicing his disapproval. No one commented on his outbursts or provided answers to why those aspects of the programs were being allowed in the process of repairing their broken bodies.

Three days after Smuthers had filed a formal, written protest, he had a visitor. Standing next to his office door was Patient X in his Marshalls jump suit holding a mug of coffee smiling as the Professor walked up to him.

Patient X offered his hand in greeting.

"Doctor Smuthers, it is good to meet you. My real name is Thomas Langston, and I'm here to brief you on what is happening with the subjects currently undergoing treatment."

"Marshall Langston, it is good to see you up and about. So you are aware of what they are allowing those kids to do?"

"Let's step into your office, and I'll explain the best I can."

Once seated in Smuthers' office, Langston began.

19

"Doctor Smuthers, I am not going to sit here and tell you I like all that is being done, even though I understand the necessity of it."

"Good God Marshall, what could necessitate allowing young adults, teenagers engage in sexual fantasizes even if it is only in simulations? And programing the nanites to stimulate them in a sexual manner during those fantasizes?"

"Doctor, the first part is simple. We, meaning the Marshalls Service, needs to insure the health of the subjects. Now we both know those kids are not in reality legal in regards to sexual consent, but they believe they are within the simulations. Now before you blow up, one thing the Medical staff is looking at is their reproductive health. We know that physically they will soon be complete and ready for the next phase of their training."

"Training Marshall Langston? What training?"

"Bear with me Doctor, I'll get there soon enough. We have to remember how those children came to be here Doctor. Being a married man yourself, can you deny that sexual activity does not make you feel more alive than at any other time, day or night?"

"Well, no, but they are children."

"Yes Doctor, and I can take you to any of a hundred worlds and if we watch carefully, we'll find young adults, children their ages doing the same thing, but only sneaking around to do it. But we also have to remember, at this time in the process, they believe they are much older, at or above the age of legal consent. Neither you nor I had any say so in the formation and passing of that law within Parliament, but as a Marshall, it is my job to enforce and respect those laws regardless of personal opinion. But we are deviating from what needs to be said."

He took a drink of his cooling coffee.

"Doctor, those individuals will become Marshalls once it is all said and done. And outside of yourself and a handful of others, they will not be known as Marshalls to the rest of the Service for some time. We have found we need people, people who are not

20

within the specifications of physical requirements to be Marshalls for undercover work. Currently, anyone who tries to secret themselves into crime organizations that falls within the height and build requirements to become a Marshall, are either prohibited or killed. None of the subjects will fit into that category."

"You're going to send them out to risk their lives after all the time and expense of repairing them?"

"Doctor do the math. Based on your own estimates in your proposal, the figures are almost astronomical per subject. But with each organization we take down, we will save countless lives and save the Planetary Union millions. How do you think the Marshalls Service can afford to pay for all of this?"

"I really haven't give it much thought?"

"Decades ago, we took down three of the greatest hackers in the universe and put them to work for us. By the nature they glean information, we cannot take it into a court, but they do open doors for us, find pathways to the top of the organizations so we can take them through legal means. They have also bankrupted several organizations simply by cleaning out their hidden bank accounts which they have never paid taxes on. It's that money which is paying for what you see here, and we have barely put a dent into the funds available to us."

"That very hypocritical isn't it for the Marshall Service to steal from thieves?"

"Certainly it is, and those involved will admit to it, but we steal from thieves to protect the innocent from thieves. Works out nicely that way."

"Alright Marshall, now what does that have to do with the children?"

"Let's take Cassiopeia, subject number one. She is below minimum height requirements, and body shape, yet with her enhancements provided by the process you invented, she can easily take down a man twice her size and weight once she has further training in martial arts. Now as for the sexual side of things, working undercover often requires a Marshall, or let's use the term agent, to provide services to those they are investigating."

"You mean have sexual intercourse with them?"

"Exactly. And this does not exclude the males either. Doctor, you live in a closed environment of study and education. But it is a cruel and dangerous universe out there. We are spending millions of credits on each subject, repairing what nature made defective, their service to the universe will be payment for those repairs and a full life. Cassiopeia was within a month of death, you have given her a life now, and yes, we are going to require her to pay for that life."

"And if she is killed while paying back the debt?"

Langston just looked at Smuthers until Smuthers realize whom he was talking too. Neither spoke for some time until Langston continued with his briefing.

"Doctor Smuthers, by now you have figured out that during the subjects simulation sex, they actually excrete fluids as if they were physically engaged outside the tanks. Those fluids are collected and tested for virality. During menstruation, the females fluids and eggs they dispose of are also tested, often against the semen the boys excrete. Having advised you of this, you must know that those tests have all came back positive, and the tests are no longer being conducted."

"Are you saying that the girls eggs were fertilized by the boys semen?"

"Exactly. Four boys, four eggs per girl. And no Doctor, the eggs were not allow to progress further than proof of conception. Again I cannot say I am happy with the end results, but again, it is out of my hands."

Neither spoke for several minutes as Smuthers thought about what he had been told so far. He finally broke the silence.

"So Marshall Langston, somewhere in here I suppose you are to threaten me about keeping my mouth shut?"

"No Doctor, that was not in my instructions, but I think it is quite obvious if you keep complaining, you'll be removed from your project, and it will end up in less capable hands."

"And my assistants?"

"They have been or will be briefed just as you have been Doctor. Like all secrets one day this too will come to light, and you will get the credit, and honors you deserve. Hopefully it will happen during your lifetime so you can enjoy them."

"Thank you Marshall. Now what is next for the children?"

"Doctor let's try to refer to them as the subjects. It does make it somewhat easier to deal with that way."

"Yes, I suppose so. So, what do you have scheduled next for the subjects?"

"In two weeks, I will be introduced to them via a sim as their new instructor. They will be advised of their true situation, and training will began while still confined in the tanks?"

"Why not wait until they are out of the tanks to do that? Advise them that is?"

"Doctor, they basically have super-human strength and agilities. If a single one revolts, cannot handle their true situation, at least in the tank they can be put to sleep, restrained without the risk of harming themselves and others, until the Psych Docs can attend to them."

"Do you think that is a possibility?"

"Do you want to risk it Doctor?"

"No, I guess not. Now why have you been chosen to train them?"

"I'm burned as far as working out in the field except for public investigations. But I too am enhanced which means once we start training outside of the tanks, I stand a much better chance of surviving the physical contact involved. Cassiopeia or Mala has

23

the ability, the strength now to snap you in half if put to the test. At least if I get banged up, the nanites in my system will immediately go to work repairing any damage, and my bone structure, like theirs can almost withstand a house falling on it."

"So the Marshalls Service is going to take on the world with six, young Marshalls with above normal abilities?"

"Right now there are twenty other subjects in stasis, waiting to see how this turns out. Tanks are being constructed and sterile nanites being shipped in via a Fleet contract. Once outside the tanks and the Psych Docs gives the green light, those tanks will be sterilized along with the nanites in them and new subjects will be introduced into them. Doctor, it is possible you'll have years of research ahead of you."

The meeting ended with Smuthers quizzing Langston on his life after being released from the process.

Introduction to Reality

The group found themselves sitting in a classroom, just the six of them, and none of them could remember how they got there. As they were talking amongst themselves, trying to get a handle on things, Thomas Langston walked into the classroom wearing his Marshalls jump suit. This got every ones attention.

He just walked to the front of the desk at the head of the class and leaned back against it with his arms crossed looking at the subjects. He never spoke as he watched them, watch him until Simon spoke up.

"Excuse me Marshall, but who are you and where are we?"

"Where do you think you are Simon?"

"This has to be a simulation since in real life, I am bed ridden and cannot speak."

Within seconds there was a chorus of voices from the other subjects echoing Simon's thoughts. Langston quieted them down so he could speak again.

"Mala, what do you think?"

"I think we are in some kind of sensory perception experiment. All of us are linked together to see how we would react to being whole instead of deformed, handicapped as we are."

"Why is that Mala?"

"Because we are able to do things we should not be able to do, feel things we should never be able to feel."

"What sort of feelings?"

Mala's dark complexion darkened as she blushed.

"Mala, are you talking about the sexual interaction between you and the others?" He asked her.

"Have you been watching us?" Gunther asked.

25

"No Gunther I have not, but others have. Others that are seeing to your welfare during this experiment. To clarify, yes, at the moment you are in a simulation and no, I am not a construct of the sim, I am a real person introduced into the sim. Please, raise your desk monitors."

Each subject raised their desk monitors to find two pictures on the screen. The right picture was of their deformed selves, and the left was as they saw themselves now.

"Raise the hand in reference to the pictures you see on your monitors as you believe you truly are in real life." He instructed.

Every one of the subjects raised their right hands.

"Good, thank you. Now what would you say if I told you all of you were wrong. That the photo on the left represents your true self out in the world?"

"Impossible!" Jefferson exclaimed.

Langston made a movement with his right hand and the view on the monitors changed showing the tanks lined up in two rows.

"Anyone know what those are?" Langston asked. "Cassiopeia?"

"Nanite Reconstruction Tanks. But my parents could never afford to put me in one of those, and they were not engineered to reconstruct our bodies in such a manner." She replied.

Langston once more moved his hand and a single photo came up on the monitors showing what appeared to be a man, with tubes running in and out of his body, and limbs missing.

"That was me a few years ago and the incident which left me in that condition killed two other Marshalls. As you see me now, you will one day see me in real life. A very intelligent man figured out how to fix a severally broken body, and I was the test subject to prove his theory. Once it was proved, the six of you were brought in, with Cassiopeia being the first. Once it was

26

proven that she could be transitioned into the process, the rest of you were introduced with Cassiopeia being held in stasis at the point she was in the process until the rest of you caught up."

He paused before continuing.

"Cassiopeia, you are correct, your parents could never afford this process to fix what was broken to make you the young lady you are now. None of your families could."

"Then what's this all about?" Robert finally spoke up.

Langston spent the next hour explaining what the program was all about and their part in it. He never hedged when he gave the mortality dates for each of the subjects pointing out that each would have passed on to the next life by this time if not for the project.

Internally Langston did not like most of what he was telling the subjects, but he also understood for them to succeed, for them accept their new situation and move on with training, they had to know the truth.

He responded to every question put to him without holding back, trying to ease the movement from what they once were, to what they are now and their futures. When he was asked about what would happen to them if they decided not to become Marshalls, his respond was open ended as he really didn't know.

"Gunther, I really do not know what the Marshalls Service will do with you if you select not to become a Marshall. You have been given a new chance at life, one that is costing millions of credits and it still has an estimated two years before this phase of the project is complete and you are out of the tanks. Don't you think working for the Service, protecting those who cannot protect themselves is worth becoming a Marshall in exchange for your life?"

"Marshall Langston, how sure can the Service be that one of us will not take advantage of our status to improve our place in the universe above those we are to protect?" Robert asked.

Langston smiled as he responded.

"Look around you Robert. Do you want the Service to send one or more of your friends after you with no restrictions on dealing with you?"

"Would they do that?" Robert inquired.

"Robert, right now other than myself, they will be the only people for some time who are physically and mentally capable of dealing with you in a one on one situation."

"You sir? Are you also enhanced?"" Simon asked.

"Simon, you saw the photo of me in a vegetated state, and once out of the tanks, you will met me as I am today. Yes, I am enhanced and considered the only Marshall that can deal with you people without risk of serious injury during training once you move into the real world."

Everyone was quiet for several minutes before Cassiopeia spoke up.

"Marshall Langston, I accept that we are new people in body and mind since we all seem to have a very good education at present. Are these our own thoughts, or is it some computer telling us what to say?" She asked.

"Cassiopeia, your words and thoughts are your own. As I mentioned earlier when describing how the process works, the micro-computer in your brain only provides guidance for the nanites working to improve your condition, and they provide knowledge beyond what you have already learned. Each of you was chosen for your intelligence. Before anyone speaks about your former condition, there are several tests capable of determining whether or not your brain is capable of absorbing the knowledge you will need in your future life. Your bodies may have been damaged, deformed if you will, but your brains were strong and functioning properly."

"So we are not being guided if you will, by any outside source?" She rephrased her question.

"No Cassiopeia, that would mean you have no free will, freedom to choose your path in life. But as I said before, you owe those who have given you this chance in life something in return. I will give you your doubt of what might happen to you if you do not accept the future put before you as a threat to force you into working for the Service, but our oaths is to protect humanity, and to cause you harm for not accepting your place, would be violating that oath."

"But the Service has robbed others to pay for our treatment." Mala spoke up.

"Yes Mala, we did, but we stole from people who were stealing from others, harming others, even causing the deaths of others so that you might live. Not a single credit came from honest people like your parents."

The next two hours were spent discussing training and other aspects of their lives while still floating in tanks of nanites in preparation of leaving them and joining humanity as whole people.

Robert finally asked a question that had been on everyone's mind.

"Marshall, what of our private life, I mean the one we are currently living."

"Robert, do you mean the interaction between yourself and say Mala?"

"Yes Sir."

"I'd say that is between you and Mala. Also outside of certain classrooms such as this, you will still be interacting with other sims as you did before. Any private interaction will still be available to you, and from what I understand, the programming is so exact, I doubt if you will ever know who was real and who was a sim."

"You mean there are real people interacting in this sim?" Jefferson chipped in.

"Yes, no, maybe, or maybe not. Just enjoy what you have at the moment."

Langston left them with that thought as he just turned away from them and walked out of the room. In reality he stepped off of a holo-pad, breaking the connection between him and the subjects. He walked to his office thinking about all he had told the subjects and how far he had pushed the boundaries of what he had been told he was allowed to say.

His own reality was that he should have told them even more, but withheld much more that in time they would learn. In his office he sat at his desk and activate his computer which was tied to the mainframe so he could observe the subjects in their simulated state of being.

They were still in the classroom talking about what they had discovered about themselves. Their conversations never became heated but there was some dissent as to their future, especially from Simon. Langston did notice that Cassiopeia stayed mostly on the fringe of the debates unless she was asked a direct question, then it seemed her replies were uncertain, hedged so as not to upset anyone.

Finally Jefferson pushed her into a verbal corner requiring her to give her base feelings on their situation.

"Cassi, you were the first in the tanks. How about it? Are you ready to spend years working as a Marshall to pay off the debt for your new life?" Jefferson asked her.

"Think back Jefferson. Do you remember what it was like before they put you in the tanks? I can, and in the short time we have been in this situation, I've lived more than I could ever have hoped for, even if it has been in a simulation."

She paused as to gather her thoughts.

"My body was broken, and I could only make noises instead of being able to speak to those around me. I can remember hearing my mother crying as she held me at night, telling me how sorry she was that I was born in such a condition."

30

Langston watched as it seemed she paused again, this time to get control of her emotions.

"Jeff, we never would have enjoyed interacting with one another before then, and if someone had used me, it would have been rape, and only the Saints would know how I would or could have reacted to it. You and I can make love, even in this sim, and enjoy the feelings it provides us based upon how our bodies should react to such intimacy. Yes Jeff, I will pay the debt because it is only right to do so. And I will not hesitate to do what is necessary to perform the missions I am given."

"So Cassi, you're going to allow the Marshalls Service pimp you out as a whore to get the goods on some sleazy criminal?" Robert asked her.

Langston watched Cassiopeia closely to see how she reacted.

"Robert, I don't believe you complained one bit when I suck your cock. And you sure wasn't calling me a whore when you had your cock in my ass at my birthday party with Gunther in my pussy and Simon in my mouth." She was smiling as she spoke.

Langston was watching for the boys reactions when Mala laughed as she interjected her own comments.

"Yeah Cassi, these boys do love to have their cocks sucked even if it is a simulation. Robert, you might feel our lips wrapped around your cock, but we also feel that cock in our mouths and if the simulation is correct, we taste your semen also once you shoot it into us. And we don't do it because it tastes good, we do it because…. Well just accept that we do it."

Langston knew why they did it, it was because knowing they were in a simulation, alone with just the six of them, they did it because they cared enough about each other to tolerate the situation.

He pulled up Cassiopeia's tank and opened the view of her inside the tank. The data running down the side of the screen showed her vital signs were just a bit on the high side of normal for

31

a girl her age. He had to remember that they thought they were actually older than they really were in the real world.

The training they had been receiving, and the adaption to their environments gave them the mental image of being two to three years older than their actual years. Langston did not like this aspect of the process, but as he kept telling himself, it was not his place nor responsibility to govern those aspects of the new lives the subjects would be living once free of the tanks.

Langston clarified the view of Cassiopeia in her tank, with her image floating in air with her arms spread out and her legs slightly spread apart. He input a command and her arms moved to her side and her legs came together as if she was standing still. He rotated her view to look at her face on.

Cassiopeia's red hair was a bit darker then normal, and it was long enough to go down to her waist as it seemed to flow in the currents the nanites made as they moved about her, dealing with their responsibilities of taking care of her. But that was the only hair on her body as it had been permanently removed from her armpits, legs, and her pubis.

He zoomed in on her heart shaped face and smiled at the freckles across her cheek boned and bridge of her nose. Then the freckles reappeared across the top of her chest. As with most redheads, her complexion and body tone was creamy in color, but a tone darker than the average redhead. Her nipples were modest sized and as dark as her hair.

Cassiopeia was slender with her hips narrower than her shoulders, and her stomach was flat without showing muscle. As he rotated her image like a spindle, her legs were well defined again without showing muscle such as a long distant runner, or a muscle builder might have from hours of exercise.

He just sat looking at her, not thinking about how she looked nude before him, but how she looked in the classroom, with shorter hair and an innocent look about her. Langston could not be sure if it was actually her or the computer, but her green eyes seemed to sparkle as she tore into the boys, knowing she was in control of the situation.

Langston began to wonder if her face, her body was in her DNA, or had the technicians modified her to meet their own ideas of what she should look like.

He brought Mala up on the monitor and examined her in the same manner as he had Cassiopeia. Mala had slightly larger breasts, but she was also two centimeters taller that Cassiopeia. Her body was near the same as Cassiopeia's only proportioned according to her height. Her black hair was like Cassiopeia's as it flowed about her. Her face was more elongated that Cassiopeia's but between the two of them, he felt Mala was the most beautiful of the two, but it would be Cassiopeia's look of innocence that would open doors for her.

He shut down his computer links to the subjects and went to work on the training schedule for after they were free of the tanks. The training they would be receiving while still in the tanks was not as physical as it would get once out of the tanks. But the muscle memory would still be as if they had learned the subjects to be dealt with outside of the tanks.

Looking at the two females made Langston think about his own situation. Even though it was voyeurism as he examined both females, he had no problem detaching himself from that aspect of what ever relationship he might have in the future with either female since he was over twice their age, even their adjusted age.

Langston went to talk with a female lab technician who had been friendly with him earlier to see what might progress over dinner.

While Langston was arranging for dinner and possible sexual relief that evening, Cassiopeia was involved in an interactive game the group had been introduced too which involved team tactics as the players fought aliens.

Mala and Jefferson were involved it close sheet combat seeing how far the simulation would let them go in their activities.

The others were busy finding female sims to enjoy for the evening. Even though the computer could detect certain things about each subject and noting them for later Psych review, it could not read their private thoughts. The debate had publicly ended undecided amongst the group, but privately they had all admitted Cassiopeia was right, and even if it was simulated sexual enjoyment, it was fun and enjoyable. They were going to take advantage of the pleasures as long as they were able too.

The next day they were once again in the classroom alone with Langston. He showed them their gross scores in the video game they had been playing, pointing out how poorly most of them had done in the game, even if their scores showed them to be experts.

At that point the base weapon, a One CM pistol appeared on their desks and after a stern warning from Langston concerning handling the weapon in the classroom, they began doing the one thing the game never taught them. That was how to break the weapon down and maintain it.

They learned the name of every part of the weapon, how to clear misfires, jams and other assorted malfunctions of the weapon over the next four days in the classroom before moving to a range.

Even though they were in a simulation, they discovered they could not just point and click and hit the targets. The weapons magazine held ten rounds of ammunition and they learned that unlike the video game, this pistol ran out of ammunition, requiring reloading and each day on the range, Langston pushed them to reload faster and faster while increasing their hits on target.

For a week they spent what amounted to nine hours each day period on the range before Langston put them into the video game not as a controller, but as an actual character in the game.

This proved interesting since now if the aliens in the game shot one of them, they felt the hit to their simulated bodies. Within the first day, every one had been hit and they did not relish getting hit a second time, even though there was no danger to their actual bodies.

During their sleep cycle, the computers fed them the entire Emergency Medicine Manual to include Field Surgery. The next day when one of the subjects became wounded, they had to be treated before the group could move on, and that person was out of play until that segment of the game was completed.

For two weeks they played as a single group without a leader except for who took charge during the game. Langston watched carefully as the boys seemed to take turns leading while the girls just laid back and followed orders. But he also noticed the girls stayed close together and seemed to work the problems better, and quicker than the boys.

Langston knew that the intelligence of the subjects would quickly adapt to the changing scenarios of the game, but he also knew how to confuse things to make them work harder.

Changing The Game

The normal progression of the game would be for them to move to the next weapon, the One CM Sub-Machinegun, but Langston added a weapon they had never seen before in the game. He added the Stiletto, the blade to the game.

When introduced in the classroom, Gunther was the first to point out the aliens in the game were scaly creatures which would make using the blade near impossible against their armored exterior.

Langston just side stepped the issue and introduced them to a video which demonstrated how to effectively utilize the blade. He noticed that Cassiopeia and Mala had slight grins on their faces when the video showed the blade being used against another human.

The girls had caught on quick that the game was about to change. It didn't take long before the boys also understood a change was coming.

That afternoon, each subject was placed in a one on one simulation with a human opponent utilizing only a blade which was made from rubber for the simulation, and for the rest of the day, they practiced using the blade. They quickly found out that their opponents fought back.

It was Robert who voiced his analysis of the training during a break with a red mark on his face from being slapped by his opponent with a rubber knife.

"Guys, who wants to bet that when we go back into the game, our opponents will be human, not aliens?" He queried the group.

"No takers here." Jefferson responded.

"Actually that makes sense." Mala added. "We're going to be Marshalls, not Marines, so who else would we be fighting if it came to that?"

Langston sat in his office observing both the training sessions and the conversations during breaks. The girls seemed to have the advantage as they were more agile, and being smaller, shorter than their fellow subjects, could get inside the reach of their opponents and strike faster, and deadlier than the boys. But this was not as uncommon as many thought.

Langston agreed with an old saying that the female was the deadliest of the species.

For a week the subjects endured the training with each day showing improvement over the previous day. At night before their sleep cycle, the bedtime activities slowed down as each subject either accessed knowledge of hand to hand fighting, or even practiced with a fellow subject.

Langston was spending long hours observing the subjects at night from his office. If one of them was engaged in extracurricular activities, he shut down that view, allowing them that tiny bit of privacy.

He had Cassiopeia and Gunther in one frame on his monitor as she was showing him how she was defeating her teaching opponent in her quarters. Once it appeared Gunther had the technique down, Cassiopeia began undressing and smiled, then winked, but she was not looking at Gunther when she did that, she was looking in the direction of Langston as if she knew he was watching, and from which direction. Langston quickly killed the feed from her quarters.

After the first week, the subjects were moved back into the game, and quickly noticed how it had changed. It was no longer aliens, but humans, and the battle scenarios were not in alien landscapes, but in urban situations, or even about space ships.

Some scenarios required them to take a subject into custody, and others, often mixed with that scenario, required the removal of sentries before they made their move on the suspect.

Langston let them work the problems for the first week without picking a leader as he was still developing his analysis of who were the natural leaders, except the girls continued to hold back and allow the boys to take the lead.

At the start of the second week of training, Langston introduced the lottery. Each subject would draw a colored ball from a box with an opening only large enough to put their hand into, and impossible to see which ball they were drawing. All of the balls were white except for a single red ball which when drawn, made that individual the leader for that days exercises.

First rule was no individual could be a leader again until each subject held the position. This forced the girls to deal with the aspect of leadership.

Simon lead the first exercise and as Langston expected, mistakes were made, and at each critical mistake, the exercise was frozen, giving time for them to analysis what went wrong and determine a new course of action. Langston would appear in the sim at this point to critique what had gone wrong.

Langston was quick to point out that this is where mistakes had to be made, in training, since the worse that could happen was bumps and bruises, but in real life, a team member would never return, killed because of a mistake.

At the end of the second day with Jefferson as leader, Langston received a message on his monitor which he did not expect. It was from Cassiopeia, and he was surprised she knew how to send such messages out to the real world.

It was a simple message: "I know what you are doing and relax. Mala and I are not afraid of leading, it's just the boys need their egos adjusted."

The next day, Robert drew the red ball. This put Cassiopeia and Mala into a high probability of being the leader on the fourth day. It was Mala.

Mala slowed the exercise down, preventing the others from rushing the game as they moved through four different scenarios with only one minor casualty, which was Robert.

Gunther drew the next red ball and he too, slowed the exercises down, taking the hint from Mala's actions with two minor casualties.

There was no need to draw on the sixth day since it was obvious that Cassiopeia was next in line.

When she received her first mission brief, she laughed and looked in the direction of Langston's view point and smiled. He had introduced a much harder scenario into the game just for her.

Langston had remembered that when the others were playing on the sheets, she was often inside the game, improving her scores until the group was introduced as a team. She used that knowledge as she moved through the five scenarios, taking the objectives with only one causality that was judged to be a flesh wound received by Jefferson as he moved from position to another.

During the after action review of that mission, Cassiopeia chided Jefferson for moving too soon, thus putting himself into a position to be wounded. Jefferson stood quietly as she calmly took a kilo of flesh, then he acknowledged that he had anticipated the command to move, and did move before ordered too.

This set the tone for the second week of exercises as everyone slowed down, waited for the commands and moved as a team. The casualty rate dropped at that point.

At the end of the second week, Langston introduced the Sub-Machinegun into the equation. After a week of training with the Sub-gun as they referred to it, they spent a week in the game, once again rotating leaders.

Langston noted that even though Cassiopeia spent more time studying tactics, there were not what he would call natural leaders in the group as they melded into a team once the leader was chosen. Soon each of the subjects spent a lot of their off duty time studying tactics from various sources. Social interactions nearly came to a halt during this period.

Once the first rotation of leaders was completed, Langston changed the game in that now there were three white balls and

39

three red balls in the container with one of each color stamped with a '1' on it. This broke the group into three-two person teams with the individual drawing the '1' as the team leader for the day's exercises. Again the rule on not leading two days in a row was enforced. This also caused a random mixture of the team so no team could get set in a pattern of who did what at any time.

As time progressed, the Five Millimeter pistol was introduced with a long session of training, then the Six millimeter Short Range Sniper Rifle was introduced. The pistol was for backup and concealment during investigations or raids, while the rifle was a support weapon.

The two team system stayed in effect for months with a new ball introduced with a '2' on it designating that person as the sniper for the team.

Once it appeared that the subjects had everything in hand, an eight millimeter and a twelve millimeter long range sniper rifles were introduced. And again the drawing of whom was to take what position was in the drawings with a red ball as team leader, then two black balls stamped '1' and '2', designating a short range sniper with the six millimeter rifle and the choice based upon the mission of the long range rifles. The remaining three subjects formed the assault team with the team leader.

Months passed as the scenarios changed from urban, to rural, to woodland, to desert, to mountain, both snow covered and woodland, with mountaineering skills being learned along with skiing.

Demolitions were taught in both constructing and disarming booby trapped devices which often caused much distress at first as if a mistake was made, that individual was classified as killed in action. No one escaped that classification during the initial days of training.

Breaks in training were taken up with classroom instruction on procedures from gathering forensic evidence to basic laboratory skills in process such evidence.

Classes over the rules of conduct of a Marshall was held with specific classes given to what a Marshall could do, or not do while undercover. It was noted that depending upon the case, the rules of conduct would be specified in the mission brief prior to the execution of the mission. A Marshall could refuse to accept the mission based upon such specifications if they felt it was something they morally could not do. There was no indication what the term morally meant, leaving that to the individual involved.

This once more brought up the aspect of the girls whoring themselves while undercover. The girls reminded the boys that they too often played amongst themselves, and that they too could be asked to whore their bodies to a subject. Male or female, in order to garner evidence.

With humanity reaching out into the stars, homosexuality, or the stigma of such activity had long since vanished from the universe. Who and the manner in which a person wished to spend their time with was a personal choice, and without choices, there was no freedom.

Here is where Langston had a problem. He had no desire to be with another man, and he did not look down on anyone for their choices, but he did have a problem with the ages of the subjects he was training.

The first to celebrate their eighteenth birthday was quickly approaching yet in real time, in actual years of life, that individual would only be fourteen. One of the crimes the Marshalls investigated was child sexual slavery.

Langston agreed with Professor Smuthers that these were just children and they were being denied the chance to be children, but on the other side of the coin was the hard fact they had been denied their childhood due to their disabilities which have now been removed.

He just tried to put it out of his mind as this was out of his control and his mission, the one he had accepted, was to train these children into killers. No, he had to stop thinking that way, he was training them to defend themselves, hopefully never finding themselves as he once did, a vegetable, with no sense of being.

The one thing he did appreciate about the subjects situation was that they could endure harsh conditions during training without injuries which would take them out of training. Even when a booby-trap exploded, killing one or more of them, all that happened was they felt the blast, then were taken back into the tanked body to rest and recover from the incident, to return later ready to try it again.

Time and time again he reminded them that in real life, there were no do overs and they were either seriously injured, or dead from the mistakes being made in training.

With their intelligence level and the fact they knew any mistake would only take them out of training for a short time, he had to keep them on the ball otherwise they would not take the training as serious as necessary.

One thing that did help keep the subjects from becoming complacent was holographic photos of the bodies of Marshalls who died in the line of duty, and even of trainees who screwed up and died. All of the photos were graphic and in colorful detail.

The group has just finished a long, single mission on a desolate moon to recover a kidnapped victim and capture the kidnapper without exposing both to the vacuum of space. It meant dealing with automated defense systems and a minefield.

Gunther was team leader for this mission and he tried to get Cassiopeia to take his place. As luck would have it, she drew the long range sniper ball and once in her overwatch position, she could advise Gunther of the situation in front of him.

He wanted to take his time on this, but they had all learned that the longer the mission went on, that more obstacles would be added to the game.

The assault team had just entered the habitat when Langston received another message from Cassiopeia, the second one directed at him.

42

"How much longer?"

Langston did not wait to see the outcome of the assault on the habitat as he left his office and went to the main control room. He at first stood back to see the views the tank controllers were seeing and focused on Cassiopeia's. Nothing on the screen showed anything different that it should show, and all communications from her to the other team members was written along the right edge of the screen.

He then looked at her sim screen and again saw nothing out of the ordinary. Langston considered talking to one of the communications technicians about communications between the subjects and outside computers, but hesitated because if Cassiopeia had discovered a way to communicate directly with him via the computers, the technicians might try to close the link, or it might cause the training to be put on hold until this situation could be resolved.

Back in his office the message was still blinking on his monitor with the group back in the classroom. Langston queued up a replay of the last thirty minutes of the mission then fast forwarded to the point he left his office and watched the mission come to a successful conclusion.

The message was still blinking, so he indicated it then typed in 'soon'.

Cassiopeia was turned with her back to him as the after action debrief was being conducted amongst the group, when she turned to look so Langston could see her face, smiled, then 'thank you' appeared on his screen.

Langston shut down his computer and left his office. What was to happen next was out of his hands as today's exercise was their graduation mission, even if they were not aware of it.

The Awakening

The group spent the next three days after their rescue mission in their tanks being fed all aspects of flight in preparation for the final phase of their simulation training.

After the three days of data feed, they were back in simulations with either single seated craft or dual piloted craft. They flew everything from basic freight missions to combat assault craft from Assault Boats to fighters.

For nearly a month, without a single day off, they flew at the controls of every known space craft and non-space capable vehicle in the known universe.

At the end of the pilot training sequence, they gathered in the classroom and waited, not knowing what was next for them. Langston entered now wearing a short beard and his hair pulled back in a ponytail, showing grey at his temples.

"Ladies and gentlemen, the time has come for you to be released from your time in the tanks and enter the real world. The training you have received will be retained once awake from your long sleep, and the information gathered by those overseeing the program will help others in similar condition as your former selves."

He just looked at them, as if waiting for a question to be asked, but none came.

"Now when I leave this classroom, the people who actually control your waking time here within the sim will close the circuit and the next time you open your eyes, it will be outside your tanks and in the real world. I have been told that each of you will take different times to process from the tanks to reality, but for you it will be as if you just blinked, while for the people who have worked for years, watching and caring for you, it will take as long as it takes."

He paused again.

"Today there are six of you, and as soon as your tanks can be sterilized from your presence, others will occupy them along with four new tanks waiting for their patients. Consider this. If the process ever becomes cheap enough for the general public, the time, the research data that your time, your bodies have provided can and will save hundreds whose quality of life is no better than yours once was. For that you should be proud of what you have achieved."

He smiled at them, then finished.

"Until we meet again."

Langston vanished from the room as the subjects also were removed by the controllers. When he opened his computer in his office he had a third message from Cassiopeia.

"Yes, we shall meet again."

He was tempted to take a final look at her in her tank, but resisted as he thought he knew what she meant by her statement, and he had to stay detached from any interaction between them, any of them.

Langston left his office to go talk to Lauren, a communications technician he had recently became close to so he could hopefully exercise a bit of his hormonal response to Cassiopeia's cryptic message.

For the subjects in the tanks, time stood still as the Psych Docs checked, then rechecked the profiles they had built on each subject. A final psych test was given to each subject for comparison to the initial test taken years before at the beginning of the program.

Several computer simulations were ran using both tests on each subject as the Psych Docs were insistent that no subject be released from the tanks until it was certain how they might react once free of the restraints of the tanks.

The final step was to release the controller's access and control of the micro-computers in the brains of each subject. There were specific, extreme protocols added into the micro-computers to insure these super-human individuals could not turn against humanity.

The criteria for activation of those lines of code were strict and even those who insisted they be added, recognized that any one of the subjects could do a lot of damage without the program being activated, shutting down the subject.

That was the key to the program, shutting down the subject, but not killing them. When Langston read the background on the added program, and what it would require for activation, he just shook his head thinking it was a waste of computer code, but it made the powers in charge comfortable.

The subjects were totally isolated from each other, but that did not matter as they were all in a comatose state as their finally medical checks were made to insure they were ready for removal from the tanks.

One of the last medical procedures preformed on the females was the introduction of birth control implants in them as it was figured that once free of restraints, they would once more become sexually active, testing how real sex compared to the simulated sex they had been experiencing.

Although Langston was authorized to view the removal of the subjects from the tanks, he chose to spend the time on the ranges as he had came to realize that he was not as detached as he should be from the subjects, one in particular.

Langston could not get over the fact that in reality Cassiopeia was still a child even though her body and mind was advanced in age. It would be impossible for anyone to hide the fact they were by date of birth, on an average of only fifteen years old, yet their minds and the maturity of their bodies was that of twenty.

This would be the final psychological adjustment they would have to make once introduced to the world at large. This was one of the things the Psych Docs had no idea how they would react too since time in the tanks, and in the simulations seemed longer than it had actually been.

In reality, Cassiopeia would be sixteen in five months, which by Universal Law, was of legal age to marry. Langston had no intention of any manner of contact other than that during training, and he certainly had no desire to marry, at least one so much younger than he was.

It would be a month before he would be reintroduced to the group, and he had that month to determine his course of action concerning interaction with the group.

As each subject was removed from their tank, they were taken to temporary quarters to be cleaned up and prepped for awakening. The nanites which had filled their lungs, providing oxygen to their bodies had been evacuated through various means as directed by the micro-computer as did those in the mouth, throat, and nasal passages.

Once each subject was clean, including their hair washed but not cut, they were taken to their isolated quarters and watched as the other subjects were dealt with in the same fashion. Even the boys hair was nearly waist length, and the Marshalls Service outlines for grooming was open enough, it was determined that the individuals should pick their first hair style once awake as a manner of giving them the image of freedom.

But isolation for each subject was just that in for the first month, no two subjects would be in proximity of another. A Psych Doc would be on hand with each subject when awakened to ensure each one would know the reason for their isolation, and to answer any questions within reason.

When the last subject, which was Mala was in her isolation quarters, a signal was sent out to all attendees to wake the subjects up from their induced comas. Since no two individuals are alike, it took nearly twelve hours before they were all awake and interviewed by the Psych Docs.

As suspected, every one of the subjects protested their isolation and demanded they see the other subjects of the program. They found such demands fell upon deaf ears.

Over the next weeks, none of the subjects left their quarters with being heavily escorted to whatever location they needed to be for whatever test or examination required of them. They were put thought every known type of physical examination possible to check their strength, endurance, and reflexes.

On the mental side they were given university level examinations covering the subjects they were given while in their sleep states to verify the retention. Their scores were above average in every category and each subject was given certification showing they had completed, and would later have a university graduation ceremony for the record.

Once those exams were completed, they were tested with both hands-on and written exams on the subjects they learned while in the sims. One test was on whether or not the introduction of nanites to their systems gave them the ability to see clearly in low light environments by having them break down a Sub-Machinegun in a near dark environment, then reassemble it within the time frame specified in the Marshalls Service Weapons Handbook.

The transition from isolation to returning to the group was interesting as Langston watched via his monitor. The setting was a Hexagon room with six doors and each entrance was a blind corridor, preventing anyone from seeing the others.

Each subject was placed in the corridors at random intervals so as not to see the others and were told to stand by the doors and they would be remotely unlocked, then to proceed through the door. They were not told what was on the other side of the door, giving them the impression this was another test, which for the Psych Docs, it was, and how they reacted beyond that door would speak of how they had adapted to their real lives.

Langston's primary view was of the hexagon classroom with smaller views of each individual waiting for their door to unlock. He noticed that none of the subjects seemed nervous or impatient as they waited.

When the distinctive sound of the doors unlocking was heard, it almost seemed like a ballet as each subject reached for the door knob, and opened the door, then stepped through it. There was a moments pause, then chaos erupted in the room as cries of joy at being reunited with the others came from every subject. Instead of going to the nearest individual, which in a hexagon room would have been confusing, they instinctively moved to the center of the room and joined in a group hug, with kisses being exchanged all around, even the males.

This went on for several minutes as the subjects reacquainted themselves with each other in full, flesh form as Langston watched, waiting for his queue from the Psych Docs to once more take over the daily lives of the subjects, or trainees as he often thought of them.

When the message from the Psych Docs ran across the bottom of his screen that he was free to interact with them, Langston shut down his computer and left his office for the kilometer long walk to the specially constructed room.

He was nervous as he covered the distance knowing that at some point he would be tested by them, especially one redhead, who seemed to be attracted to him. But he was concerned how that attraction would affect her training when he announced that he was marrying Lauren, taking him out of the picture as a possible sexual partner.

Langston walked down the nearest corridor to the door where he would make his entrance and paused, took a deep breath then opened the door. The noise was now subdued as they talked amongst themselves, making jokes about each other's real bodies, and he could hear one of the boys commenting about when they could get together after hours.

He stood and looked at them in silence as it seemed they had not noticed him entering the room thinking he had to change his image of them since they were not children anymore, but young adults.

Simon noticed him and called the group to attention with them reacting as they should from the previous training they had received. Every one of them had turned to the direction Simon had been looking, towards him as he stood there, watching them.

He only spoke two words to them. "Follow Me." And turned back and out the door. He never looked back to see if they were following.

Outside was a twelve passenger air-van waiting for them. He indicated them to board the vehicle as he took the front seat next to the driver. Once all were aboard and the door secure, the driver lifted without orders and headed for the groups new quarters and training area.

There were few muted comments from the back of the van as they flew far from the complex they had been staying at out over fields of grain growing beneath them. It was nearly two hours before they landed at another, smaller complex in front of a group of buildings.

Langston got out and the group followed his lead. He stood looking at them as they lined up in no specific order, nearly shoulder to shoulder waiting for his next instructions. He never spoke to them as he turned away and walked towards the large building they were in front of and entered it.

He walked almost to the center of the building's large, open room. He turned back to them and waited as they once more took a formation in front of him.

"Alright people this is how it is. You will notice along that wall is your bedding. You have to assemble your own and place it where you wish within this room. There are also lockers needing to be assembled for your things. On the opposite wall is everything you will need during your stay here. The equipment bags are marked with each of your names, and in them are all your uniforms and other items needing to be put away. The crates contain your personal weapons and equipment, which means you will have to assemble your equipment vest to your liking."

He paused for a moment.

"Behind me is the sanitary facilities and your kitchen/dining room. You will fend for yourselves during this phase of training, cooking and keeping the entire building clean. If you need something for maintenance, log it into the computer in the dining room. If you wish something special for chow, log it into the computer. Make note here people, that computer is only for official use and is coded to prevent any activity other than that. So don't try to send messages to your family, or anyone else you think should receive one."

He tried not to look at Cassiopeia, but could hardly miss the crooked grin on her face.

"In the kitchen area is a large pantry already stocked based upon your food choices while in the sims. The nanites you carry now in your bodies are the remains of those you were floating in and they tried to insure the flavors you were tasting were as exact as possible, but you will find some foods, especially since you will be preparing them, will not taste the same. Be prepared for that difference."

"Also specific sanitary supplies for the females are in a cabinet within the sanitary facilities. Now as you have obviously noticed there are no walls, or dividers within this area, which is your bunk room. You will also notice upon assembly, that the bedding is not designed for the comfort of two people."

He paused to let that sink in some more before continuing.

"Unlike the sims, your quarters within the sims, there are no cameras to observe your activities inside this building. How you deal with associating with one another after hours is left up to you, but be warned, lights out at 2200 hours standard time, and anyone found outside these quarters after that will find themselves with a load of tranquilizer, as there are automated intrusion sensors and tranquilizer rifles situated all around this compound. Don't risk being found lying in the dirt the next morning."

He once more paused.

"That is all I have to say at this time. You are free to take care of business. Dismissed."

At that they ganged up on him, with the shaking of his hand and hugs, even from the males. He was expecting Cassiopeia to make some subtle move on him, but he was surprised when Mala kissed him on his cheek, then whispered in his ear.

"I'd really like to suck your cock."

She then stepped back and grinned at him. He replied to the group instead of directly to her.

"Another thing I forgot to mention. You have two days to get yourself organized, which includes making up a duty roster for the kitchen and such. You will be all alone here during that time as I am heading back to the Processing Complex to get married. My quarters are across from here, and are restricted to only myself and my bride unless you are ordered to go to them. Now I have to leave and watch the next group of subjects be placed in their tanks to begin their program which you have just completed."

He never spoke another word but did notice both Mala and Cassiopeia had looks of slight disappointment on their faces before they passed from his view. As he was flying back to the main complex, he had to laugh at the thought of no privacy in their quarters considering the activities they had while in sims. But knowing the difference between the sims and real life, it would be interesting to see how they dealt with it.

Back in the barracks, it was quickly noticed that there were no tools to assembly their beds or lockers until Simon reminded everyone of the tool kits they carried in their vests. Soon they were dug out of the boxes, then everyone went to work getting their beds and wall lockers assembled.

Once they had their beds put together, mattresses and linen included, they turned to the lockers. After that it was time to break out the equipment and get it stowed along with their uniforms. There was no order to who would sleep in what bed, but Cassiopeia took the last bed away from the door and Mala took the bed next to her.

Mala grabbed Robert and they went to fix the midday meal as the rest of the group went about insuring the barracks was cleaned up from the debris of unpacking the bed and things. After the meal, they started putting together their equipment vest with Mala's and Robert's items laid out on their bunks as they cleaned up after the meal. No one seemed to notice how long it took for the pair to clean up after the meal except for Cassiopeia.

When Mala returned ahead of Robert, she was smiling and drinking a fruit juice. She handed it to Cassiopeia, and then sat down on the bed looking at her. Cassiopeia gave her a look to tell her more.

"Cass, the pantry is a nice place for some things beside food, and the fruit juice helps cut the after taste, after tasting them."

Mala licked her lips as Cassiopeia laughed. She took a sip of the fruit juice, handed it back to Mala and went back to work putting her gear together. Robert returned to his bunk a few minutes later with a slight grin on his flushed face.

Cassiopeia looked at Mala again and Mala seemed to read her mind.

"It doesn't taste any better in real life as it did in the sims."

Again Cassiopeia laughed and continued her work as Mala started putting her gear together.

Once the basic gear was assembled and fitted, they turned to putting together their simple assault packs including a single field ration from the pantry. Cassiopeia held back and caught Jefferson in the pantry and found out that Mala wasn't lying as she returned to the bunks sipping on a different fruit juice with Mala laughing knowing what Cassiopeia had done.

Simon and Jefferson fixed the evening meal and had the dishes and such cleaned up in just a few minutes compared to Mala and Robert, but only Cassiopeia noticed that minor time difference.

Everyone gathered on two bunks, facing each other and talked about the experiences once out of the tanks. They also speculated on what type of training they would face now isolated from the rest of the planet with no method of leaving the area except for on their feet.

Just before lights out, Cassiopeia and Mala tore their bed covers from their beds then drug their mattresses out into the middle of the room and stood looking at the boys. The boys caught on quick as the girls began undressing with all of the mattresses being laid into a formation large enough for all of them.

Cassiopeia stepped onto the middle mattress and pointed to Robert who was already nude.

"You put that thing in my ass tonight and I'll feed it to you for breakfast. Never again, understand?"

"Yes, Cassi, I understand."

"Boys enjoy tonight because it is the only time we will play in this manner." Mala commented before she kissed Cassiopeia as she pulled her down onto the mattresses.

As this was happening in the barracks, Langston was consummating his marriage to Lauren.

Live Fire Exercise

The girls were still sore on the third morning when they fell out for physical training with Langston standing before them. They did not realize that the feelings during the sex while in the sims came from nanites stimulating the vaginal nerves, but they had never been stretched out inside as they were during the orgy. Even the boys who played with each other during the night felt the soreness of their actions.

Langston took them for a ten kilometer run passing the ranges they would be using and at the halfway point they met the air-van where they drew their basic weapons. This added the weight and bulk of the weapons for the return run back to the barracks.

At the barracks, they were told to tear down the weapons, clean and lubricate them before they showered and had breakfast. When he was asked if he would inspect the weapons once cleaned, he put it back on the group. The group would inspect themselves remembering that if a single weapon failed at a critical moment in a fight, every member of the group was at risk, therefore it was vital that they take care of each other.

Just before he released them to deal with their weapons, he told them while they were out, a communications device was mounted by the exit for them to use to communicate with him while he was in his quarters. Once they had completed all the details given and ready for the next training mission for the day, to buzz him.

In the showers, Gunther made a move on Cassiopeia who told him to jerk himself off because she had better things to do than blow him this morning.

The rest of the morning was taken up with a law class, updating the information they had already received. Their instructor was presented to them in the classroom via a holographic image, holding to the principle of no other physical contact with outsiders other than Langston. Even Lauren was advised to stay away from the students if she was outside of the quarters.

Langston did not like the fact that Lauren was in a sense a prisoner of her new home, but she understood the importance of the contact rule.

After the midday meal, Langston took them out to one of the fire and maneuver ranges where ammunition was available and put them through the course seven times, changing leadership each time through the course. All travel from point to point would be at a gentle run, building up their lungs to match the muscle they had already developed in the tanks.

He worked them till it was past the normal meal time, but did not give them a chance to break into their field rations. Langston never commented on how they did on the range that day as he just sent them back to the barracks to clean their weapons before showering and a late meal.

Even enhanced, the day was long and wore on them as they quickly cleaned their weapons, then themselves before eating a light meal. Simon was the first to notice that Cassiopeia seemed distracted when he snuggled up to her in the shower and kissed her neck. She just stood there as if nothing happened, but when she did turn towards him, she just stood, letting the water rinse her body, ignoring him.

Cassiopeia just cleaned herself and left as Mala was bent over letting Jefferson take her from behind. It wasn't long before all of them noticed she was distracted, as almost in a trance as she moved from the shower, to dress for the evening, then to eat. Later as she was lying on her bed, Mala finally got her attention.

"Cassi, what's going on with you?"

"What do you mean Mala?"

"In the shower, Simon came on to you and it was as if he wasn't there. Before, he was one of your favorite lovers. It seems since we left the range you have been off in another world."

"Sorry Mala, I've been reading, or actually my computer has been reading to me."

"What have you been listening too?"

"The Fleet Marines Tactical Operations Manual. Have you noticed, we are not being trained in Law Enforcement as we are being trained as a tactical operations force. A small, elite force to tackle those missions normal Marshalls are not trained to or capable of dealing with."

"Cassi, have you compared what you are thinking to the Service Manual?"

"Yeah Mala, I have, and against the Planetary Union laws concerning the use of the Fleet in Law Enforcement. The use of Fleet personnel is limited in such matters, and it almost seems as if the Union's criminal element is taking advantage of those limits."

Cassi rolled over to look directly at Mala.

"Mala, while in the tank, I was able to access the main frames and found Langston's file. He was, is one of the best the Service has ever fielded, but the people he was after used hired guns, mercenaries, former Marines against him and his team. He was the only one to survive, but was considered a vegetable until Professor Smuthers developed the process that was used to being him back alive, then make us whole."

Cassiopeia sat up and looked over Mala's shoulder at the boys who were gathered together talking.

"Yes Mala, I like Simon about the same way you like Jefferson, but we cannot allow ourselves to become distracted with our new, found pleasures of the flesh. There are two of us and four of them. If we allow it, they will use us every night, and at times in between. I cannot, and will not tell you how to enjoy yourself, but even contact with each other has to slow down, and slow down a lot otherwise we are going to become too attached to them, and they are going to take advantage of us."

"Cassi, do you really believe that?"

"Did Jefferson ask you if you wanted to have sex in the shower, or did he just come up behind you, rub himself against you, then bend you over?"

"Frack! I just let him take me without thinking about it. Cassi I enjoyed it, but you're right about them coming at us as they do. Was the group sex a mistake?"

"Yes and no. I'll not get into my thinking on that just yet, but I think any interaction of any nature between us and them should be a reward for them, not just because they have an erection. That also goes for us enjoying them or each other. Mala, I can't be any clearer than that."

Mala sat for a time just thinking about what Cassiopeia had said before breaking the silence.

"How hard is it to get your computer to access such things as the Marine Manual?"

"Do you talk to yours much?"

"No, not really. It does remind me when I need to drink something, or it seems I am stressing my body by telling me to correct my position, otherwise, we rarely converse."

"Mala, it's an AI, not just a computer. Talk to it, you'd be surprised what it can do. I learned that in the tank while in a sim. Talk to it and let it help you as mine has helped me."

They were still talking when the lights went out and Mala leaned over and kissed Cassiopeia good night. A few minutes later, Gunther came to Cassiopeia's bunk to see if she would be agreeable to a few minutes of pleasure. Cassiopeia sent him away disappointed. When he turned to Mala, she did the same.

Mala was lying on her bunk trying to communicate with her micro-computer in a manner that would benefit her as she was opening that pathway as Cassiopeia had spoken about. She went to sleep thinking that if Cassiopeia could do it, then she also could manage it.

The next morning there was a light rain and the run was rough as the road was unimproved, just dirt, and the mud made things interesting as they ran in the rain. Once again it was clean the weapons, then the body, before eating.

Cassiopeia went into the pantry and took four ration bars from the stock, putting two in her pack, and two in her accessory pouches in her vest. It wasn't long before everyone was in the pantry, doing the same thing. Robert went to the computer and inputted a resupply of the ration bars to ensure they had an amply supply.

Back out in the rain with a dry uniform on and only their floppy, wide brim bush hats to keep the rain off their faces, what little good that did. A ten kilometer run to the combat course they were to run, with climbing obstacles place through the course. Everything was wet and slippery especially once they maneuvered through several crawling obstacles. Nothing escaped the mud.

When they returned to the barracks just after dark, everyone except Cassiopeia tried to scrape as much mud off their boots as possible. Everyone yelled at Cassiopeia when she just walked past them and into the barracks tracking mud in with her. Gunther watched her walk through the barracks from his vantage point and saw she went directly into the sanitary facilities.

"Yoah! Cassi has gone into the showers!" He yelled at the rest of the group, then entered and followed her muddy footsteps to find Cassiopeia standing under a hot shower, letting it remove as much of the mud from her body and weapons as possible.

After a few minutes under the showers, Simon grabbed a toilet cleaning brush and began scrubbing his weapons, loosening the mud even more, then went after his boots. Others began doing the same thing and passing the brushes around since the supply was limited.

Cassiopeia took her vest off, then her battle jacket and once she felt the jacket was clean enough, she laid it down on the shower floor and began removing the things from her vest pouches, laying them on the jacket so she could clean the vest, especially the pouches which had collected mud. Everyone copied her approach in getting things cleaned.

Soon, everyone was nude in the shower with no attempt to play, just get clean and warm after being in the cool rain all day.

Cassiopeia was the first one finished since she had started before the others and made two trips to her bunk with her gear, and a trip to the uniform refresher to let it finish cleaning and drying her uniform.

She was still nude when she took a bucket from the utility closet, filled it, then stepped out into the barracks and poured the water on the muddy floor. She did this four times along the muddy tracks from the door, then got the squeegee used to clean the shower floor and began pushing the mud and water into the shower to let it thin out under the showers, and flow down the drains.

Simon and Robert grabbed mops and began mopping the floor behind Cassiopeia to get up the remains the squeegee missed. Soon everyone was working to clean up the mess from the entrance to the showers before they turned to their weapons and gear.

Robert announced he was going to make soup cups so they would have something hot in their stomachs as they began to work on their weapons. He made a large pot of vegetable soup and placed it on the floor at the center of the bunks so each individual could refresh their cups without having to go into the kitchen.

Cassiopeia and Mala just put dry panties and field bras as they worked on their gear and the boys put on briefs. As soon as the refreshers announced dry clothes, they put their vests, hats, and the uniforms they had been wearing that morning in to get them clean and dry.

They were still working at getting their gear back together when the automatic system turned out the lights in the barracks. Mala gathered up the remains of her things and took them into the sanitary facilities where the lights were always on, but dimmed to finish up what she was doing. Cassiopeia and the others soon followed her.

No one spoke as they finished getting their gear ready, and when Robert began to gather the soup pot and cups, Jefferson and Mala helped.

The next three days were repeats with the rain and mud, but the course of live fire changed daily. They were told to take a day off, gather their strength and relax. Both females passed on sex that night leaving the boys to wonder what was going on. When Simon suggested that the girls were taking care of each other, Gunther, who had the bunk next to Mala told them that wasn't happening, and pointed out neither were ever alone with the other.

During breakfast the next morning, Jefferson acting as the front man, put the question to the girls.

"Cassiopeia, Mala, what's going on? In the sims, and when we first got here, we had sex any time of the day. Now nothing."

Mala shoved a large piece of ham in her mouth and nodded to Cassiopeia, who wiped her mouth and looked at the boys facing them.

"First of all, let's get one thing straight. We're not whores for you boys to play with when you get an erection. I know that sounds weak considering all we have done with each other, but in the sims, it was just play. It was a freedom which we had never experienced and truthfully, the experience was great. No concerns, no worries, just go for it and enjoy the moment. So in a real sense, we were whores in the sims."

She took a sip of hot tea.

"But now things are different. Sure, we took advantage of that first night to see if what we felt in the sims was what real life felt like, except in the sims, we didn't get sore from the usage."

As she paused to gather her next words, Simon spoke up.

"How are things different?" He asked.

"This is no longer a game we are playing. Mala and I both agree we have favorites amongst the four of you. Favorites only in that if I decide to have sex, I would approach that person first, but it has always been good with each of you. But ask yourselves, why are we here? Everything we have done here, we did in the sims, only now, we are flash and blood and have live ammunition. We've passed all the written and verbal exams to qualify for the title of Marshall, yet we are still in training. For what?"

She paused to let that sink in.

"Have any of you tasked your AI's to learn more about what we are doing, or why we are doing it?"

"We can do that?" Gunther asked first.

"Look, I know I've had my AI longer than anyone. I was alone for months before they even tanked all of you, and I spent a lot of time talking with Tia."

"Who's Tia?" Mala inquired.

"Tia is the name I gave my AI. Good grief, didn't any of you try to talk with that thing in your head?"

No one responded to Cassiopeia's question.

"Okay, okay, we'll get back to that." Cassiopeia commented. "Let's start simple here people. Ask your AI's to give you the data on the Marshalls Live Fire Courses. You'll find that what we have been doing is not in the books. But if you ask for Fleet Marine Live Fire Assault Courses, you'll see that is basically what we have been doing all the way back into the sims."

Cassiopeia sat back a bit from the table, looked at her plate then forked a couple small pieces of green vegetables into her mouth as the others just sat looking at her. A couple of the boy's looked as if their eyes had glazed over a bit as they were getting a download of information from their AI's. Finally Jefferson broke the silence.

"Frack! We have been running military assault courses!" He commented.

"We're supposed to be Law Enforcement, not a military tactical unit!" Gunther exclaimed.

The comments went on for several minutes with Cassiopeia just eating more of her vegetables with a piece of ham from time to time until everyone calmed down and seemed to focus on her.

"Alright Cassi, so they are turning us into a Para-Military group. What has that to do with our after hours fun and games?" Simon asked.

She took a drink of tea before responding.

"Simon, have you ever considered how we, Mala and myself, feel an hour after you pound yourself into us? Yes, pound. Sure it feels fantastic while you are doing it, but then later the soreness starts. It's not much when one on one which is why neither of us wants to play the free for all like we did our first night here. But when its all said and done, we are still reminded by the soreness in our crotch of the fun and games, while you go off to sleep, or whatever else you want to do."

No one spoke as she forked more meat into her mouth, waiting for them to comment. It was Mala who spoke up.

"She's right Simon. We might be enhanced in many ways, but as great as it feels at the moment, we still have a price to pay. Then if one of you fills us full in the morning, we have to contend with the leakage all day, which is sticky and uncomfortable."

Cassiopeia giggled as she tried to swallow the ham in her mouth before further commenting.

"Guys, she's right, but now here is my reasoning for not opening up every time one of you have an erection. The more we interact in such a manner, the closer we all become. The feelings we have for one another now is from our interaction in the sims, and that we all came from the same place. I'm not sure what love feels like, but I would like to think I love all of you."

"Now having said that, I'm not going to get any deeper involved with any of you, Mala included because if we really are being trained as a Para-military team, it's going to be hard to loose a single one of you, and we all know that is possible. Getting closer will make it worse. So just because you have an erection and my bare ass is close by in the shower, don't be bringing it to me to deal with. Soap up and let the shower drain take away your problem. If I feel the urge to enjoy a cock inside of me, I'll select the one I want, and when I want it. No further debate on the subject is welcomed."

With that she got up from the table and took the remains of her meal to the disposal, then the plate and flat wear to sink for later cleaning. As she was doing this, she heard Mala echo her comments.

Cassiopeia was sitting on her bunk when Mala sat down on her bunk, facing Cassiopeia. Cassiopeia had her eyes closed, looking at diagrams her AI was displaying on tactical movement of small units.

"Cassi?"

"Yes Mala?" She responded without opening her eyes.

"How do you talk to your AI? I mean it is a computer."

"Mala; talk to it as if you were talking to me. Yes, it's a computer, but it's an AI. They respond in kind."

"Cassi, it sounds like I'm talking to myself when it responds."

"Then give it it's own voice so you will know the difference, especially when you are deep into something which might cause you to ignore their advice or warnings."

Soon all of the boys were sitting either on Mala's bunk or Cassiopeia's, asking for advice and testing their AI's. Everyone was so focused on what they were doing, on what they were learning they never realized it was nearing lights out until Cassiopeia made one final test of her own AI's capability. She knew she had contacted Langston's computer without the controllers being aware of it, but could she contact the other's AI's?

She instructed Tia, her AI to send a message to the others at five minutes before lights out warning them of the time. There wasn't much more for her to do, but to sit quietly as she waited for the clock to run down on her instructions.

Cassiopeia was watching her team mates as the clock hit the mark. Suddenly they all seemed to come alive, with Robert scrambling backwards off Mala's bunk in surprise of what has just happened inside his head.

"Damn Cassi!" Gunther exclaimed.

"How'd you do that Cassi?" Mala asked.

"If our AI's can communicate with the main frames to gather information, why can't we communicate with each other?" Cassiopeia replied.

"What are the range limitations on this ability?" Jefferson inquired.

"I don't know Jeff. Before I only talked to another computer while in the tank. I have no idea how well this will work, or what limitations we might have on it. But I do know that I was able to bypass the controllers when I used it in the past. They never discovered I was communicating with another."

"Another? Who was you talking too?" Simon asked.

Cassiopeia never responded to Simon's question, she just stood and began undressing for bed. The others took the hint and moved away to their own beds. Mala sat down on Cassiopeia's bed once she was in it and leaned over to her as if to kiss her, but instead whispered in her ear.

"It was Langston, wasn't it?" Mala asked.

"Mala let it drop. He received my messages but never responded. It was just a childish crush. Now go to bed, tomorrow will probably be a long day back in training."

Mala kissed her as if they was going to climb in bed with her then moved off onto her own bed.

The next morning when they exited for their morning run, they found two things on their small porch. One was the leadership container and the other was a medium size shipping container. Jefferson and Robert brought the shipping container into the barracks and opened it.

Inside the container were six battle helmets, each with a tag telling which helmet was for which member of the group. The girls had to let their hair down so it would properly fit on their heads, then figure out the best way to wear their hair since both had hair nearly to their waists. Without guidance from Langston, they had not cut their hair.

The good thing about the helmets, the face shields had an electro-static barrier which prevented the rain from coating the shield and disrupting their view. The bad thing was that the helmet would allow water to run down into their uniform if they did not attach the extended collar which also restricted air flow to the neck and head. The small blowers in the helmets helped some in keeping the head cool, but they could be overwhelmed, especially if in a chemical environment where they shut off and sealed to protect the wearer.

There were stencils and paint in the container so they could stencil their names on the helmets, but they all decided they could do that after the evening meal. Exiting the barracks, they all drew a ball from the container fixed to the porch railing, with Gunther drawing the command ball. This was back to the single formation as practiced in the sims.

Cassiopeia was the first to find she could link her AI directly to the helmets AI and advised the others to do the same. During the run, Cassiopeia played with the capabilities of the helmet since they had never used them in the sims, and found she could track each person's pulse and respirations.

Watching Gunther's vitals, she could tell he was nervous about being in command. He was smart, and aggressive as a team member, but he was a little insecure in command. Later as they were showering from the run, she moved to him and pressed her body to his and whispered in his ear that all he had to do was relax and remember his training, and if he would do that, and get through the day without screwing up, she'd blow him once lights were out.

She kept her word to Gunther that night.

Three days later, Cassiopeia drew the red leadership ball and broke the group into three-two man teams. She pulled Jefferson as her team mate, Mala and Gunther together with Robert and Simon as the last pair. The teams ran side by side for the run and then went through the live fire exercises as partners with Cassiopeia sending movement instructions, often with diagrams to the pairs during the exercises.

That night the group sat in a circle in the middle of the barracks as she taught them how to utilize the helmets AI coupled with their own AI's to provide real time guidance and instructions to one another.

For a month they ran exercises regardless of the weather and on five different occasions, ran exercises through the night, taking the next day off to rest. The ration bars coupled with the field rations got them through the days and nights without a problem of hunger distracting them, plus the ration bars provided addition energy they need to stay with the program.

Mala and Jefferson put their mattresses together across the other side of the barracks and slept together one night knowing they had the next day off. Cassiopeia stayed celibate as they all noticed she was lost in her connection with her AI learning more and more about weapons and tactics.

Cassiopeia was also ahead of the game when they began carrying explosives during training and utilizing them to take out obstacles. They were taking a break one afternoon when Simon brought up the obvious.

"Every few days these ranges change, even if it a minor change. How is that?"

"Engineers are coming in at night while were are in the barracks and changing them. That's also one of the reasons they are so far from the barracks so we will not hear them working. Look over there, you can seen where their transports have sat down." Cassiopeia replied as she pointed across the road at the depressions left by the transports in the ground.

Langston was always present, always watching how the group functioned. He was also wearing a battle helmet, recording their actions for later review. What he never told the group was that time was running short for them as far as training was concerned, and if the Marshalls Service determined it was time, they had a team mission ahead of them. One he was not being allowed to participate in, as he would soon be going back to the Project's Complex to begin training the new batch of students in the tanks.

The Fortress

The group was called to the classroom where they waited with Langston at the back of the room. They sat patiently for the large screen in front of the room to activate and tell them what was next in their program. Having figured out how to communicate using their AI's, they talked amongst themselves without a sound or movement, giving away their personal thoughts and concerns.

When the screen activated, the group saw a distinguished looking older gentleman sitting at a desk wearing the tunic of a Marshall with stars on his shoulder boards. His first words were not directed to the group.

"Marshal Langston, you are dismissed and instructed to return to the Project Complex to take over the training of the new subjects. I'll give you a moment to say your goodbyes to these people."

The group turned to look at Langston as he moved towards the door, stopping before exiting.

"I'm honored to know you, one and all. I'm sure we shall meet again, but until then, take care and watch each other's backs."

With that he was gone. The group turned back to the screen.

"Marshall's, I am Director Griffin of the Marshalls Service, and I have a mission for you."

The view on the screen changed showing a walled estate, set on a hill. Then the screen broke into several views with the Director in the middle view.

"This is the estate of one Victor Scarborough on Leary. He is known to run a criminal empire operating in eight planetary systems. His crimes are various, yet we have been unable to remove him from the estate and his guards. According to all the reports on your team's training, we want you to bring him to justice."

No one commented as the Director shifted some papers and the views of the estate changed again.

"For this mission, the team leader will be Robert Barnett, and…."

"NO!" Robert interrupted the Director.

"Excuse me?" The Director spoke again.

Robert stood up.

"I said no sir. With this being our team's first mission, it is only right that Cassi, I mean Cassiopeia should lead this mission, since she is the oldest of the group in training."

"Are you dictating terms to me Marshall Barnett?"

"No sir, only expressing how I feel about the leadership of the team on its first mission Sir."

Every one stood except for Cassiopeia.

"Director, I agree with Robert." Gunther spoke up.

The rest of the team echoed Gunther's comment.

"Marshall D'Auber, what are your feelings on this?" The Director asked Cassiopeia.

Cassiopeia stood and looked at her team mates before speaking.

"Director, there isn't much to say is there? If this is what the team wants, then I don't see I have any choice, and neither do you unless you can convince myself, and the team, that there is a valid reason for me not to lead this mission." She responded to the Director.

"I'm not sure I like your tone Marshall D'Auber."

"Sorry Director, it's the only tone I have in these circumstances. Or have you forgotten that I have only been mobile and vocal for barely a year, therefore my social skills may not be up to what you are used too, Sir."

It was easy to see the complexion of the Director slightly redden from the exchange of words.

"So it looks like I appoint Marshall D'Auber as team leader, or I have a mutiny on my hands here." The Director finally spoke again.

"No Sir, we'll follow whomever you select, but we feel Marshall D'Auber is best choice for our first mission, Sir." It was Mala who responded to the Director's mutiny statement.

No one spoke as the team waited for the Director to respond.

"Everyone take your seats. Marshall D'Auber, everything we have on Scarborough and the estate will be sent out to you to build your plans from. A computer will be set up at your location to receive updates and submit your mission plan. Do not delay."

With that, the screen went blank leaving the team to ponder what they had just committed too. Cassiopeia finally stood and just walked out of the classroom with the others following. Back in the barracks, she dropped her gear at the foot of her bed, then laid down, staring at the ceiling.

Mala sat down on the edge of her own bunk looking at Cassiopeia.

"Cassi?"

"Yes Mala?"

"Are you scared?"

"Any one with good sense would be scared. Aren't you?"

"Yes, but I trust you to get me through this first mission."

Cassiopeia never replied to Mala, she just closed her eyes and told her AI to wake her in an hour and drifted off to sleep. An hour later she awoke to find Mala still sitting, watching her. It was quiet in the barracks as Cassiopeia sat up to see all of the team on their own bunks looking in her direction.

She stood and looked down the row of bunks.

"Strip your vests, double check everything. If you think it might fail the next time in the field, notate it and we'll make a resupply request. Robert, thank you for your trust in me, but you're still in trouble. You're my number two. From first look at the target, we'll work in twos. Jefferson, you're with me. Robert and Simon, Mala and Gunther. Pair up and go over each other's gear. Mala, you handle logistics on this. Double check our field rations and make sure we have three packs per person plus eight ration bars per person. If you think we need anything else in rations or such, get them ordered. Let's get busy folks as time might be short."

Jefferson grabbed his vest and headed to Cassiopeia's bunk as she picked own up, and began emptying her pouches on the bunk. Jefferson followed suit, using half her bunk space as she used the other half.

As Mala was in the pantry inventorying rations, Gunther emptied his vest, then gathered Mala's and copied what Cassiopeia and Jefferson was doing. He looked at Mala's things, let out a light chuckle then went to the pantry and told Mala to insure they had feminine products available, not knowing when the mission might take place. She laughed and just placed the order without checking the cabinet in the sanitary facilities.

It was just before the midday meal that a team of technicians arrived with the computers and printers for the team to begin building an operations plan. With them was a Marshall who said he was from the Security Division of the Marshalls Service and he had brought maps, and other hard copy items for them to utilize. He had Cassiopeia sign for a large document case, then gave her the code to unlock it without it destroying the contents it contained.

As soon as the technicians left, Cassiopeia moved their operation into the classroom and went to work studying the estate and information provided to them.

Scarborough had five servants plus a butler in the house. It was stated there were ten mercenaries acting as outside security. Scarborough was known to have a single mistress that lived with him, but might have one or two additional females in the house at any time.

No matter how Cassiopeia looked at things, her original idea of two person teams held. But the one thing she had to work out was getting inside the estate walls to tackle the house itself.

It was the non-combatants what concerned her. How would they react, and how to deal with them. The mercenaries would be live targets without concern, but the servants were a different problem.

Neural dart pistols became the answer for the servants. Each pistol contained five darts in a self-loading magazine. The darts sent an electrical current through the targets body, incapacitating them within micro-seconds. The only drawback to them was range as the target had to be within twenty meters, and the thickness of the clothing they were wearing.

Cassiopeia had Mala add six dart pistols to the needs list plus a total of three magazines per pistol. The pistols would be worn on their vests, and their One CM pistols would be worn in leg holsters.

They spent three days going over how to assault the estate, getting over the estate walls before turning to how to get to the estate. From there they refined how to deal with the walls as they had to move forty kilometers through woodlands to the jump off points for the assault, carrying everything they needed for the assault.

It would be up to the Marshalls Service to get them to the initial drop off point then pick them up once it was over. Cassiopeia was concerned about removal, especially if they did not totally eliminate Scarborough's security element. One individual could create havoc as her team was being removed if they had the right weapons in hand.

Everything was rechecked, the suppressors on their weapons had been replaced. Helmets were checked to insure full charges in their power packs. Packs were emptied, checked then repacked. Medical supplies were checked with extra blood plasma replacement fluids added as a precaution.

Cassiopeia had spent long hours going over the estate and available diagrams of the estate manor until she felt she could navigate it in the dark with her eyes closed.

They had a written and signed document authorizing deadly force against anyone that hindered their passage which included Scarborough, if he could not be taken alive.

Cassiopeia submitted her plan and included a note to the logistics portion of the plan for an extra full set of magazines and ammunition to be provided on the transport to Leary, plus the pouches to carry them in. It would take a bit of rearranging each persons gear, but she wanted that extra ammunition in case things went sour.

Once the plan had been acknowledged as received at the Marshalls Headquarters, she shut everything down and headed for bed. It was passed lights out when she entered the barracks and found her mattress now on the floor between hers and Mala's bunk, with Mala's mattress also in the floor with Mala waiting for her there.

Cassiopeia removed her clothes and joined her on the mattresses. After the first long kiss, Cassiopeia leaned her head back from Mala and gave her a questioning look as the taste of her lips and tongue spoke of earlier activity.

"Gunther." Was all Mala said, then kissed Cassiopeia again.

Later as Cassiopeia fell asleep with her head on Mala's chest, Mala had her AI contact Cassiopeia's telling in to insure she slept, even past the time it normally awoke her as she needed her rest. Tia, Cassiopeia's AI agreed, then Mala let herself go to sleep.

The next morning, when Mala awoke with Cassiopeia still lying on her, she found they were covered with one of the light blankets. Later she learned that Simon had covered them during the night when he got up to use the toilet.

Two days later they received the order to Stand By for pickup. A shuttle landed four hours later and took them to a Marshalls Service transport craft for the trip to Leary.

It took five weeks to transit to Leary and during that time, the team exercised daily and went over the plan until even Cassiopeia felt they were wasting their time. Each individual had their own small quarters on the ship and Cassiopeia broke her own rule and entertained each member of the team once during the trip with Mala spending several nights with her, often just talking and sleeping together without becoming sexually engaged.

The drop went as planned as the shuttle left the transport as the transport did a fly-by of the planet instead of taking orbit. The shuttle would sit in the initial point until the call came for the team to be picked up.

Mala and Gunther took the point since they had the furthest to travel to their assault positions. Cassiopeia and Jefferson were next, then Robert and Simon. Visual contact was not necessary as their helmet's AI kept everyone advised of the other's positions in the movement.

Everyone was in place by three in the morning, but as Cassiopeia examined the estate from her vantage point on a small rise, she did not like what she was seeing. She pulled up the views from the others and it was as if the security force inside the estate had at least doubled. It was also unknown how many more might be hidden away. The last intelligence on the estate was less than forty-eight hours old and it did not speak of an increase in security.

"Ghost Team, this is Ghost One. Abort, I say again, Abort. Gather at my position for further orders, Over."

Each member responded according to their assigned numerical position on the team. Cassiopeia waited for the next call via a small relay satellite which had been placed in orbit, relaying their communications to the transport which would have moved away, but ready to return as needed. The requirement for the relay was for official recordings of the mission.

"Ghost One this is Stennis, do we copy you are aborting the mission, over?"

Stennis was their transport.

"Affirmative Stennis, the target has been reinforced, and I'll not risk my team going against it, over."

"Standby your location Ghost One, Out."

"This is Ghost one, standing by, out."

It took nearly an hour before all of the team members were gathered at Cassiopeia's location. They all agreed from thermal tracking by their helmets, there were too many people they could detect behind the walls to tangle with them without losing people.

As they just relaxed and watched the estate, three shuttles suddenly dropped onto the open ground between them and the estate. At first Cassiopeia thought it might be a heavy assault force, but when then first shuttle discharged its human cargo, it did not lift, and the individuals began walking towards where Cassiopeia and the team were in hiding.

Cassiopeia's AI advised her the IFF's on all three shuttles identified them as Marshalls Service shuttles.

From the angle the team had on the estate versus the shuttles, the gate of the estate opened and men poured out as a casual walk, heading for the grounded shuttles. The shuttle ramps dropped, and the men boarded the shuttles as three men walked from the closest shuttle towards them.

"Cassi, why do I think we've been had?" Simon asked what everyone, including Cassiopeia was thinking.

"Stay in place and be ready for anything." She ordered then stood. Everyone was spread out so she was not worried that a

76

burst of fire at her might take out others as she started walking towards the men walking towards her. She told her AI to enlighten the men and amplify. The man in the lead was the Director of the Marshalls Service.

Cassiopeia's Sub-machinegun was hanging across her body as she stopped and waited for the Director to come closer. For a second she thought of shooting him for what she felt he had done to her and the team, then let the thought fade into obscurity as she was sworn to defend the law, and killing the Director would violate that oath. But she was pissed.

The Director and the two men accompanying her stopped about two meters from her. She told the helmet to raise the face shield so her face would be exposed to the Director. With her left hand, she pulled a small flare from her vest, activated it and dropped it onto the ground to her side, illuminating her and her visitors.

"Care to explain this Director?" She spoke in a harsh tone.

"Langston said dealing with you would be an adventure more than the others. He also warned me that picking Barnett as the original team leader would cause problems for the team, but he left the reasons unanswered. Marshall D'Auber, this was your graduation exercise. We were concerned that once on site, even faced with an overwhelming force, you'd still attempt to complete your mission. Congratulations on making what we all feel was the correct decision."

"Director, and if I had ordered the attack? What about those people inside the walls? What of them?"

"Marshall, the moment you gave the order, we would have counter-manned it. To be honest we were very nervous for several minutes waiting to hear your call."

"What now Director?"

"Marshall D'Auber, once my shuttle lifts, your shuttle will pick you up here and return you to the Stennis. You will return to your training area and in doing so, with the help of your team, write a new field training program for those who will follow in a few years. We have ten individuals in the tanks at the moment and twenty five in stasis waiting their turn."

"So we write up a training program, then sit on our asses?"

"Cassiopeia, I understand you are upset and your tone is showing it. Get ahold of your emotions here before I start taking it personal. No, we will find work for all of you either as a team, paired teams, or individuals. One or more of you might even return as trainers for the new people, but you are too valuable to just let sit around gathering dust."

"Sorry for my tone Director. Is that all Sir?"

"For now, yes, but know that we agree with Marshall Langston in that all of you have a bright future ahead of you in the Service. We'll meet again Marshall. Rest up as you might find yourself very busy later on."

He never waited for a comment as he turned and headed back towards his shuttle followed by the two other men with him who had not spoken during the meeting.

Her team gathered around her as she watched the shuttles leave. No one spoke for several minutes as they waited for their own shuttle. It was Gunther who broke the silence.

"I can think of a lot less expensive ways to hold our final exam. I have the feeling that what is waiting for us down the road could get downright nasty."

During the trip home, Cassiopeia only slept with Mala once and Simon once, otherwise she stayed to herself, thinking about how far she had came since entering the tank. Mala spent the first week entertaining all of the males, one a night until she had enough, then except for sleeping with Cassiopeia that one night, only slept with Jefferson as they grew closer.

It took nearly seven weeks once back at their barracks to write up a training program, testing it, then rewriting it before they felt it was as good as it could be.

During that time, Cassiopeia sent Langston a message via her own AI to stop, or slow down the sexual aspect of interaction of the tanked subjects. She said it was a distraction that she felt was too easy to fall into outside of the tanks. This time Langston responded to her message advising her the controllers accepted her thoughts on the matter and had taken steps to do as she advised.

Over the next two years, the team recovered three kidnapped individuals in high risk situations with only one of the team injured. Gunther's leg was nearly severed just below the knee when a booby-trap exploded. His internal nanites prevented him from bleeding to death, and once evacuated, he returned to a standard tank to have his leg repaired. He was out of action for nearly a year.

Cassiopeia and Mala spent two months undercover as lesbian lovers working a young girl trafficking case for prostitution. But Cassiopeia's biggest case was just around the corner, and it was one she knew she should turn down, but took it anyway.

The Working Girl

Cassiopeia was standing behind the pilot watching the screens as they were slowly closing with the fleeing luxury yacht carrying the man they were after. Xeno Fillage was a drug smuggler by trade, but when he dipped into politics and arranged for the Chancellor to be assassinated, the Planetary Marshall's decided he was now their business. The assassination failed, but the Chancellor was wounded, and two of his aides were killed in the attempt.

For the past six standard months, Cassiopeia had been undercover in a Nibiru brothel gathering information on Xeno through the other whores and clients. She had finally nailed down where he was hiding, and the regular Marshall's raided the luxury resort he was staying just minutes after he lifted off planet. Now the chase was on across the galaxy to bring him to justice.

It was Cassiopeia's compact yet curvy body which had made her perfect for the uncover part of a whore, a prostitute. With her orange/red hair and emerald green eyes, she attracted a lot of clients. That plus when word got out that she had zero inhibitions concerning making her clients happy, they paid the additional price for the time spent with her. She had her own, personal Med-Tech which she checked clients for diseases. It also read their DNA and compared it to Xeno's since the word was he had been surgically altered. But Cassiopeia would only admit it too herself that she enjoyed the time in the brothel, but she was constructed to be a Marshall.

Outside of the Marshalls Service highest echelon, only the Chancellor's and his Judicial Council knew of the Marshall's like Cassiopeia, origin and oath which was directed to only the Planetary Charter. They could not be bought or induced to violate said charter and anyone, to include the Chancellor, would bring down their wrath if any attempt was made to alter their conditioning. Even those who tried to change it through legal means found themselves under the scrutiny of the Marshall's.

Marshalls like Cassiopeia could be killed since they were human in form and function, but barring mishap, they could live for over one hundred and fifty standard years before age began to take its toll on their bodies. They healed fast from all but the most major of injuries, and it was said their mental capacities exceeded the smartest of the intellectuals in the universe. And their bodies belied their physical strength which was on the average three times greater than a man their size. Their immune systems were strengthen to protect them from poisons and biological agents that might be used against them. In private, those that knew about where the Marshalls came from often called them Supermen.

Cassiopeia watched as the yacht entered the Tantus system where it launched an escape pod towards Tantus 3. The only readings they could get on the pod showed it contained one human passenger.

"Cassi, get ready to drop. You get the person in the pod, and we'll continue after the yacht." The pilot spoke without taking his eyes off the monitor.

"Yes Commander, feed the planet data to my pod and I should be ready in two minutes." She spoke as she turned to leave the bridge for her pod.

The pilot fed the planets data to her pod and it loaded her kits and weapons based upon the planet's ecology. Cassiopeia was out of her jumpsuit even before she entered the launch chamber and put on the dark greens and blacks of her jungle clothing, stepped into her boots, then into the pod. She was strapped into her pod when it began a ten second countdown to launch. Cassiopeia read the planetary data from her monitor during her descent as it also fed the information to her battle helmet's AI along with the location of the escape pod in relationship to the settlements on the planet. Her pod adjusted it's descent to bring it down within five hundred meters of the other pod. The landing spot was in dense jungle inhabited by flora and fauna, which if not cautious of, would kill any human it came in contact with.

81

Cassiopeia felt the drogue chute deploy as the monitor indicated via a camera to inspect and insure it was properly functioning. Her descent indicator showed her pod gradually slowing as it passed through the planet's atmosphere until the primary chute deployed. She could see from another monitor the jungle canopy rising to greet her, then felt the small retro-rockets kick in for three seconds to further slow her descent.

She braced herself as her pod crashed through the massive growth of trees, bouncing off tree trunks as large as three meters in diameter, tearing through limbs thicker than a man's torso until the retros kicked in a final time just before she came into contact with the planet's surface. Cassiopeia found herself hanging face down in her pod, suspended by her restraints and reached out to the control panel to activate a righting sequence which would put her upright and on her back again.

The pod did an automatic scan of the surrounding jungle for any life form that could be a danger to Cassiopeia when she exited the craft, then emitted a high frequency sound, far above human hearing, to dissuade any creature from staying near the craft. Cassiopeia watched the control panel as the exit indicators turned from red to green with a flashing yellow light advising her of caution.

Cassiopeia hit the restraint release and bent over to retrieve her battle helmet from between her legs at her feet. Donning the helmet, it automatically linked to the pods AI and she watched its internal monitors upload all of the planet's data, then indicated its AI was ready to proceed. Her own AI, Tia echoed the ready status of the helmet. She reached around the sides of her decent seat, recovered the straps to her weapons belt, fastened it, pulled her One CM pistol, checked to insure it was ready, then reached out and pushed the hatch opening control.

It was dark under the multi-layered jungle forest canopy even though her helmet's AI was showing it was midday according to planet time. Her helmet automatically adjusted its vision to night observation, and the terrain around her became lit up with a golden hue. She exited the pod and squatted twice to loosen her body from the effects of riding the pod as its hatch automatically closed. Moving around to the side of the pod, she opened a hatch and removed her pack and One CM rifle. Within a minute, she was ready to move on to complete her mission.

Due to the lack of sunlight at the surface of the jungle, there was little vegetation to slow her movements or hide creatures which could do her harm. Her helmet's AI was scanning her surroundings for animal and insect life that was potentially dangerous to humans as she moved in the direction of the other pod with help of her AI.

Cassiopeia had landed at a straight line distance of six hundred and thirty-eight meters from her objective, but the rough terrain of the jungle floor extended that to nearly one thousand meters, and it took her almost six hours to reach the pod. The pod's hatch was still open and the interior was crawling with insects and indescribable creatures. Her AI was able to link with the pod's AI and downloaded its survival equipment lists before the pods power ran out. The pod's passenger fit the description of Xeno and he was armed. Cassiopeia compared the pod's information to the tracks left in the soft soil, then started her pursuit of her target as she sipped water and nutrition supplements through the tubes inside her helmet leading back to her pack.

For two planetary days Cassiopeia followed the tracks noticing that they were becoming less sure in step, and found blood on several leaves of ground plants matching Xeno's DNA. He was hurt and slowing down. At night, she had erected her survival shelter which would give her protection from harm as she slept and rested. She was in no hurry as she knew she was gaining on him with each step. And unlike a normal human, she only needed four hours of sleep.

Cassiopeia had seen Liger tracks crossing the tracks she was following, but they were old, and when she came upon some that were fresher than his tracks, she knew that she would only take Xeno alive, if she was very lucky.

At midday on the third day she discovered the remains of Xeno's body and his pack. His rifle was nearby and showed to have fired over a dozen shots before it appeared to have been torn from his grasp. His body was ripped apart and partially eaten where it lay, and one leg was completely missing, probably taken for eating at a later date. His pack was ripped open but its contents contained data chips which her AI scanned, and advised her that they most likely contained information on his entire operation.

She took several DNA samples, gathered up all the evidence available to include insuring the AI had taken photos of the body and ripped open pack from every angle before plotting a course to the nearest village. Batesville was forty-three kilometers away and her AI estimated it would take almost a planetary week to reach it based on the terrain she had to traverse.

During her trek, Cassiopeia was attacked twice by Ligers, but her AI gave her sufficient warning. She had to kill one, and was able to frighten off another. Cassiopeia took the twelve centimeter fangs from the one she killed as a souvenir.

It was close to midday when Tia, her AI, advised her of an incoming communication from Mala's AI, Peter. This surprised Cassiopeia since there had never been an attempt to communicate in this manner over such a vast distance across space. Tia said the connection was weak, but once they reached the top of the ridge Cassiopeia was climbing, the connection might become stronger.

At the top of the ridge, Cassiopeia took a break and had Tia make the connection with Peter.

"Cassi, this is Mala, are you copying me?

"Yes Mala, connection was weak, but stronger now. Where are you?"

"I'm home, at the compound. Cassiopeia, I have some bad news. Simon is gone and Robert is in the tanks."

"What happened?" Hearing Simon was gone felt like someone had hit her in the stomach.

"They went after a gun runner, who got the jump on them. Simon took a twelve millimeter in the head, Robert took him out, but received several hits to the torso from the same weapon. I'm really sorry Cassiopeia, I knew you liked Simon."

"The critter must have had warning because they were too good to make a mistake, giving the other side notice."

"Yeah Cassiopeia, that thought has been mentioned."

"What about you Mala? What's on your schedule?"

"That's the good news. Jeff and I are getting married, and the Director has put us in charge of the new trainees here at the compound. We're off the assignments roster."

"Mala, that is great news. Listen I still have a long distance to travel, so I best get moving. Give Jefferson a big kiss for me, and I'll see you when I get this job done."

"Be careful Cassi."

As she walked, she thought of Simon and how tender he was when alone with him. Even back in the sims, he would often come to her sim room and they'd just talk for hours about all manner of subjects giving the others the image of them engaging in sex. Yes, of all the boys, then she corrected herself, men that she trained with, he was her favorite.

She also thought about the ripples that Mala and Jefferson may have made when they announced to the Service they were getting married. Just because they were constructs did not mean they couldn't find love and be loved.

Cassiopeia had to stop and raise her face shield to wipe her eyes of the moisture that was leaking from them. She had fell in love once with a man twice her age who was now married, and her feeling for Simon were nearly the same. She wondered if she would ever know true happiness. Had the controllers learned of her feelings and altered her conditioning? She just lowered her shield and continued her journey.

At mid-morning of the ninth day, she came to the buffer zone of Batesville and just stood inside the jungles edge surveying what was in front of her. Her AI linked with a communications satellite, then sent a message that she was safe and where to pick her up when transport was available. Cassiopeia stepped out of the jungle and stood for a moment so the spotter in the observation tower over a kilometer away would see her before walking towards the tower and soy bean fields in front of her.

Any person walking out of the jungle into the village is suspect, because no one travels the jungle alone and survives. The jungle is infested with animals that will eat a person without killing them first, and other things that can kill you, but too small to eat even a finger. Then there are the parasites that can infest the body eating it from the inside out.

So when the village was established, the settlers pushed back the jungle a full kilometer back from the fields and the village itself. Even with that buffer, danger still existed, so any person walking out of the jungle was suspect of harboring evil spirits.

When the spotter noticed a human walking out of the jungle, he called back to the village to alert the protector of the human's presence. The protector arrived on his tri-wheeler as the human was still crossing the buffer zone. He watched the human move with a casual cantor to their pace as if this was completely natural for them. Looking through his monocular, he noticed that everything being carried on the person was arranged in a military like manner with a rifle hanging diagonal across the body ready to use with a pistol down the right leg at the reach of the hand. Another pistol was on the vest the person was wearing as was a long knife hanging upside down on the left side. The clothing was of a cloth he could not identify at this range, but what bothered him the most was the head was completely covered by a helmet with a gold face shield which prevented him from any type of identification.

Cassiopeia watched herself being watched as she crossed the plowed ground between the jungle and the crops. The tall man who had arrived on a tri-wheeler just stood below the watch tower, watching her move to where she was thinking on setting up camp for the night.

Even with amplified vision thanks to the helmet, she could not get a good look at this man since he was holding a monocular up to look at her, but his free hand held an old fashion shotgun which could still do her grievous harm if turned on her. She figured she needed to make some indication she was no danger to them.

He watched as the person walked up to the edge of the buffer and stopped. They reached behind their back retrieving a long-bladed knife, attached it to the rifle, then unhooked the rifle from the vest and stuck the rifle into the ground by the bayonet where it was retrievable, but out of the way. They dropped their pack and begin unpacking it. Within minutes a tent was up and anchored into the soil. They opened a seam in the tent and tossed the pack in and followed it in and resealed the seam. The rifle was still stuck into the ground, but the protector knew the person still had two pistols in the tent.

His real job in the village was as a carpenter, but he had been elected as protector after the last one was crippled by a liger attack. He knew he had to approach the tent, but even a man of his size has fears, and he knew he was being watched by not only the spotter, but others that had followed him out from the village. He clutched the old twin barreled shotgun to his chest and slowly walked to the tent stopping about five meters from it.

"Hello the tent." He tried not to yell too loud and waited for a response. What he got took him completely by surprise as the tent flap opened and before him stood the owner, only wearing black panties and a black field bra. She stood about a half meter shorter then him, and had close cropped orange red hair. Her lips were full under bright green eyes and as he took her all in he felt himself stirring in his pants. She smiled and her teeth were white and orderly in her mouth.

"And who might you be?" She asked. Cassiopeia evaluated him in a second. Over two meters tall, muscular, grey just beginning to touch his hair with a neatly trimmed beard. His clothing was simple as such was normal in a frontier town and his boots were scuffed from work. He had what appeared to be the remains of wood chips clinging to his light jacket and a metal star on his chest. The way he was holding the shotgun told her he was nervous which was dangerous to her situation. She had to calm him before she made any specific move.

"I'm Thomas Jefferies; I'm the Protector for Batesville, the village just up the trail." He spoke slowly.

"Well Protector Jefferies, I am Lieutenant D'Auber, Planetary Marshalls Service. If you will relax, I will get my identification disk."

He nodded and she turned, bent over into her tent, exposing her pantied backside to him. He felt himself nearly jump through his pants at the sight of her bent over that way. She stood, stepped out of the tent with her identification in her hand and walked up to him. He took it and tried to focus on the disk, but now he could smell her musky odor. Looking at her, he saw she was looking down at his crotch and the bulge in his pants. She looked up at him and smiled, licking her lips while her green eyes sparkled.

"What are you doing in the jungle Lieutenant?" He was trying hard to focus on his mission.

"I was chasing a criminal that was wanted for high crimes against the Union. It seems one of your ligers got to him first, so I came to the nearest village before calling for transport." She smiled and once more looked at his crotch. "Protector, are you married?"

"No, I am not, why do you ask?"

"Because your erection needs a place to empty itself before it tears a hole in your pants." Her words were soft and alluring. "I'll be here until tomorrow. Come back later when there are not so many people watching us. I've not taken a man for nearly a full cycle, and you appear to be all man." She took her disk from his hand, turned and walked back to her tent, entered and sealed the flap leaving him wanting to grasp her firm ass with his hands.

Jefferies shook off his stupor and went back to his tri-wheeler. It was uncomfortable with his erection, but by the time he arrived at the crowd that had gathered near the spotter's tower, he had softened and shrunk so not to be obvious. He made his report to the crowd and told them to go about their business as he was going back to his shop to finish the cabinets he was working on. He spent the rest of the day trying to focus on his work, but the sight of her kept invading his mind until he finally gave up and went into his house to take a shower.

Cassiopeia sent a message advising she was ready to be picked up and that Xeno was now in the stomach of a liger. She cleaned herself up utilizing the premoistened towelettes they carried, then fixed a bite to eat.

She thought about the Protector and recognized she had over played her hand with him, but if he came back, she would make the night interesting. Her mind went back to Simon and she just sat cross legged on her sleeping pad and softly cried for him.

Just before dark Jefferies stopped at the spotter's tower and told the spotter he was going to check on their visitor. This time he took his tri-wheeler up to the tent and noticed the rifle was still in front of the tent. Even before he stepped off the vehicle the tent flapped opened inviting him in. As he stepped in the tent, she was lying on a pad, naked and inviting. Jefferies sealed the tent and began removing his clothes. Her legs were open inviting him to enter her as he finally became nude, but as he stepped towards her, she closed her legs and shifted her position so he could lie beside her.

The air in the tent was cool and there was a pleasant fruity fragrance in the tent. Her lips were now painted a deep red making them look ready for a night of passion. He lay down beside her and pulled her too him. Her lips found his and within moments they were wrapped around each other as each lusted for the other's body.

Before she blanked out all other thoughts, she wished this was Simon who about to make love to her.

They spent the evening in each other's arms in a dance of lust. He took her twice that evening which surprised him and pleased her. The moons were up and full when he left her tent with her breasts marked, and he carried bite marks on his chest. Never before had he had a woman so full of lust.

Jeffries stood next to the spotter's tower at mid-morning as the scout boat lifted taking Cassiopeia back to where she came from. Word had already spread that he had spent the night in her tent and he didn't care. The two women in the village he often took to his bed might be mad for a while, but they would get over it and return to his bed when they wanted him inside of them. Jeffries returned to his shop and finished the cabinets he was working on.

Revolt

The trip back to the Compound on Magnus, was uneventful for Cassiopeia as she stayed to herself, away as much as possible from the crew taking her home.

Home she thought, consisted of a large, one room bunk area with no color or style, on a planet she wasn't even born on.

They had taken a defective little girl on the edge of death and transformed her into what she was today. And the only thing she could think of was that she had become the very thing she was afraid of becoming, a whore who would spread for a man just to have the feeling of closeness.

That was the only excuse she could make for taking Protector Jefferies in her tent. She had lost Simon, gone from her life, and she just wanted to feel the closeness that making love provided. But now, a week out of Magnus, she felt dirty.

Working in the bordello was business, work as it was as she was looking for a criminal. Granted, once a client proved they were clean and not Xeno Fillage, she gave them their monies worth, and privately admitted she enjoyed doing it. This also scared her.

For two days she isolated herself in her quarters as she just lay on her bed, and considered where her life was taking her.

**"Tia, what did the controllers, the programmers do to me while in the tank? How did they alter my personality?"

**"Cassiopeia, I do not understand the question."

**"Is it normal for a woman my age to have such desires?"

**"Cassiopeia, I still do not understand the question. What desires are you speaking of?"

**"Tia, research sexual desires and inhibitions. It seems I have to force myself to refuse or deny myself sexual contact. From all of my contact with other females, unlike myself, they seem to have points they will not cross during sex, even the prostitutes I worked with on Nibiru, yet I had none of those. Did the programmers block or removed those inhibitions while I was in a coma in the tank? You were there, you were active in my brain at that time. Research and report."

**"Cassiopeia, this will take some time."

**"Understand."

Cassiopeia let herself drift off to sleep as Tia searched for the information she had asked for. Tia's awakening of her was gentle as always.

**"Mistress, I am sorry, but there is a block on the information you requested that I cannot by pass."

**"Is there any indication who placed the block?"

**"There is only an indicator giving a Marshalls Service Memorandum. It gives the Memorandum number and date, but not the title and again, I am unable to access it."

**"Thank you Tia. Please log this search and keep the Memorandum information available."

**"Yes Cassiopeia."

Cassiopeia had to smile as she had once tried to get Tia to call her Cassi, but Tia said her programming did not allow that level of informality. She lay there for a time then had a thought.

**"Tia, connect me with Mala if possible, and check for any manner of listening or recording of our conversation please."

**"Yes Cassiopeia."

It was a few minutes before Cassiopeia was connected to Mala.

"Hey Cassi, Peter says you want to talk."

"Mala, I know this might be a touchy subject, but have you ever given any thought about your sexual conduct?"

92

"Cassi, you mean dropping my panties when and where I wanted too, or the boys wanting me too?"

"Something like that. I know you've been out on missions, single, undercover missions, but did you get laid during those missions, outside of what was necessary to do the job?"

"Yes. Cassi I found myself dropping my panties for any man who paid me the necessary attention without thought. I screwed half the crew of the last transport I was on before I realized what I was doing. You?"

"Close, but I'm fighting the urges right now. I think the programmers messed with us while in the tanks."

"Cassi, I told Jefferson about those times, and he said he had problems too. We're hoping that being married will shut some of that down."

"When is the new group to be released from the tanks?"

"I think they have about seven weeks left in the tanks, then the month of adjustment before coming out here. What are you thinking?"

"I'll be home in a week, I'll talk to you then."

"Alright Cassi, see you then."

The connection was broken between them, then a minute later Tia spoke to Cassiopeia.

**"Mistress, I could not detect any ease dropping on your conversation."

**"Thank you Tia."

When Cassiopeia arrived on Magnus, she was taken directly to the Project Complex where she was given a complete physical as per Service Regulations for any Marshall who was either undercover or involved in hostile terrain which she qualified for both. She was then taken before the Psych Docs for a full Psychological workup to determine if she had been affected by her experiences while in the field. The old term of Post-Traumatic Stress Disorder was no longer used, but the effects were still watched for, especially in Marshalls working high stress cases.

After two hours of the Docs asking her questions, with her non-responsive, just staring at them with no emotion on her face, they began quoting her regulations stating she was required to answer the questions.

She had Tia give her the Memorandum information.

"I'll make you people a deal. Give me a hard copy of the Marshalls Service Memorandum 57 Dash 920177D as in Delta, concerning the programming of my mind during my processing in the tank, and I will answer your questions. Otherwise, shove it where it hurts the most."

"Marshall D'Auber, that is classified information which you are restricted from accessing." The Doctor who had identified himself as Cooper responded.

"Doctor Cooper, I am aware of that, and my AI, the one you people stuck in my head, is also restricted from accessing that information along with other items concerning my construction, my repairs in the tank. Put up or shut up as the old saying goes."

**"Mistress, the Doctor activated an alarm. Security personnel are on their way here now."

**"Thank you Tia."

"Do I frighten you Doctor Cooper?"

"What do you mean by that Marshall D'Auber?"

"Well, you activated an alarm which is summoning security. Since this meeting is being recorded, let it be recorded that I mean no harm to any person or persons here today, nor tomorrow. I just want answers. If you wish that I be restrained, I will not resist, but one thing you have to consider is that you will not get an answer from me without my questions being answered. I've said all I intend to say on the matter. I'm done here."

Cooper sat and looked at Cassiopeia, then scribbled a note and passed it to a Doctor Powers who nodded agreement. Cooper rose from his seat and moved to the door and opened it. Outside were four Security Agents, posed and ready for a fight if needed.

"Marshall D'Auber, go with these men please."

"Certainly Doctor Copper. Where are we going?"

Cooper turned to the agents.

"Take Marshall D'Auber to Room 403 please, and stand by as she is prepped for a tank."

Cassiopeia laughed as she stood.

"Four agents for little old me?" She turned somber. "You should have summoned twice that number to have a fighting chance, but as I said, I will not resist."

She walked to the doorway and looked at the Security Agents.

"Well let's go boys so you get a good look at me while I strip for the tank. But no touching, or you will lose a hand, or maybe an arm."

As they walked to the Prep Room, Cassiopeia talked to Tia.

**"Tia, I think they are going to try to bypass you and get into my brain. Can you prevent that from happening?"

Tia was silent for a moment.

**"Yes. Once the nanites from the tank enter your body, I can gain control of them by linking them with those already in your system. I will need to pull some in to build a wall between the new one and myself. The extra nanites in your head could give you a headache from the increased pressure."

**"Do what you have to do but to not let them in my brain to change my thinking. To make me conform to their way of thinking."

95

**"I'll do my best Mistress."

When Cassiopeia entered Room 403, she walked directly to an IV stand, took it in her hand as if to pick it up, but instead using her thumb, pushed against it, bending the stand over into a right angle as the Security Agents watched with their eyes wide and nervously fingering their weapons. She just laughed and began to undress, smiling at the men as the clothes came off her body.

Two hours later she was being lowered into a tank of nanites under the watchful eyes of Doctor Cooper. Just before her head became submerged in the tank, Cassiopeia turned her head towards Cooper, opened her eyes, then winked at him.

Cooper ran to the control center as Cassiopeia was supposed to be in a medically induced coma after the drugs she had been given and the vital signs that were taken before introducing her to the tank.

In the control room, he looked at her vitals and everything read in the norm, but then the tank data began to show odd readings. He had the tank technician pull up the odd data in the tank and when it was analyzed, it showed the drugs she had been given being expelled from her body via nanites.

Suddenly the speakers in the control room squealed loudly, making everyone cover their ears to protect them, then it stopped. Next came a voice. The voice of Cassiopeia over the speakers.

"Play your games all you wish Doctor Cooper, but until I get my answers, you'll never receive yours. You people created me, created a Frankenstein monster if you will, and I can leave this tank anytime I wish. For now I'm going to relax, and just let time pass me by."

The reading on the tank went wild for a moment and when they looked at the visual monitor of the tank room, there was a hand made from nanites extending above the tank with the fingers folded over except for the middle one. Then it collapsed back into the tank and all of the readings flat lined as if there was no one in the tank.

As they were trying to gain control of the tank, Langston entered the control room.

"Doctor Cooper, did you need to see me?"

"No Marshall Langston, what ever gave you that idea?"

"I received a message on my office computer you needed to see me immediately."

Before Cooper could respond, Cassiopeia once again spoke through the speakers.

"Thomas Langston, if you are not aware of it, there is a classified memorandum concerning our programming that I believe is detrimental to the program."

"Who is this?" Langston asked.

"The one you never responded to when I was being reconstructed all those years ago."

"Cassiopeia?"

"Yes Thomas. It seems since I refused to answer the good doctors asinine questions, then challenged him concerning the memorandum, he has tanked me thinking he can pry the answers from me. Or even terminate me if he feels I am a danger to the Service."

Langston turned on Cooper.

"You threatened to terminate her?"

"No Marshall. No, I never said a word about termination!"

"No Doctor I doubt you would have out loud, but that is an option, is it not?" Langston replied.

"Marshall Langston, you have to understand, Marshall D'Auber was undercover for nearly a year, part of that time was as a prostitute in a bordello, then she was alone on a frontier planet for nearly a week or more. We have to determine her stability just as we have to do every one who has been in those situations."

"What is this memorandum she spoke of?"

"I'm sorry Marshall, but you are not cleared for that information."

"Cassiopeia, what is the memorandum you are talking about?"

"Thomas, I do not know, even my AI cannot access it, but it does have a file number. It is 57 Dash 920177 D as in Delta."

"Thanks Cassi. Doctor Cooper does this memorandum also apply to the subjects currently in the tanks?"

"Marshall, you are not cleared for that information." Cooper once again advised Langston.

Langston walked over to one of the technicians and laid his hand on the man's shoulder and leaned close, but spoke with authority.

"Get the Director of the Marshalls Service on the line, and do not even hesitate a second."

"Yes Sir." The man stammered out.

A few moments later a woman appeared on the communications monitor.

"The Director's Officer, this is Isabella, his Secretary speaking."

"Isabella, this is Marshall Thomas Langston. Please advise the Director we have an emergency here are the Project, and I need to speak to him."

"Yes Marshall Langston, I will let him know."

The screen went blank except for the shield of the Marshalls Service being displayed on it. It was only there for a couple of seconds before the Director was on the monitor.

"Thomas, what's the problem?"

Langston explained the situation the best he could and gave the Director the file number for the memorandum twice to ensure the Director had the correct file.

"Okay Thomas, this was done by my predecessor, let me take a look at this for a minute."

He read the document on his monitor and as he read, Langston could tell the Director was not happy with what he was reading. Finally the Director leaned back from the monitor.

"Holy Mother of all Saints! Doctor Cooper, I see you standing back behind Marshall Langston. You get Marshall D'Auber out of that tank immediately, and if a single hair on her head is harmed....."

"Director I'm alright, in fact I'm safer in here than out of it except for that damn technician that keeps trying to lower the temperature in the tank."

"Marshall D'Auber?"

"Yes Director, it is I, Cassiopeia D'Auber at your service."

"Okay, I'm confused now, but Marshall D'Auber, you will be released from that tank, and turn yourself over to Marshall Langston who I place in charge of your care and welfare until I get there. And that's an order Marshall."

"Yes Sir. I will obey your orders Sir."

Thirty minutes later Cassiopeia stepped out of a hot shower, washing away the remaining nanites that had stuck to her skin, then put on a clean uniform jumper. She walked into the adjacent room where Langston was sitting, waiting for her.

"Cassi, I've scanned the room, no bugs, no cams, it is clean. Now talk to me how you accomplished what you did today."

"Thomas, the AI's they put in my head, our heads, are more powerful then they ever imagined. Granted they are still restricted by certain parts of their programing, but other than those few bits and pieces, they can do anything a major main frame can do. I don't fully understand it, but I'm going to use it where it needs to be used."

"You learned that in the tanks, didn't you?"

"Partially, yes, but only recently have I learned more about them."

"Tell me what set you on this path today."

Cassiopeia sat down and told him everything without leaving out a single piece of perversion that she had taken part in and enjoyed. She told of her own feelings concerning everything of that nature and how it was starting to affect her thinking.

She ended the tale with being honest about her crush she had on him for a long time.

"Thomas let's be honest, I never really knew my parents, and the closest I came to knowing or remembering them is bits and pieces of my mother. So you were in many ways my father figure and well, I guess more than that for some time."

"Cassi, I thought so. It was why I married Lauren other than the fact I do have strong feelings for her. Do you know she is expecting our first child?"

"Oh Thomas, that is fantastic! Congratulations, but what took you so long?"

"We wanted to be sure what we had could last."

They just talked for over an hour until the Director walked into the room.

"Marshall D'Auber, tell me what has caused this emergency?"

Once more Cassiopeia told her story to the Director as she told it to Langston. He sat quietly as she spoke, never interrupting her as she spent over an hour talking, adding things she had not mentioned to Langston. When she finished, she was specific on the verification of what she was saying.

"Director, I will return to the tank under your supervision so they, the technicians can access my AI, Tia, and verify everything I had told you. This is a sick life I have been forced into without my permission. I want out of it before I am worthless as a human except for a man to shove his cock in."

The Director looked at Langston.

"Were you aware of this situation?"

"Sir, I saws things as Cassiopeia's team instructor I felt was wrong. I sent memos forward asking about their conditioning, but never received a solid reply. I should have pushed harder for an answer, but after today, I see that I would not have been given one."

"And Marshall D'Auber, your AI, Tia is it? It cannot correct your condition?"

"No sir, Tia has a block in her programming preventing any change placed in me by my original conditioning. That is where she found the file number you were given. It was in there as part of her protocol, sir."

"After I got off the line to you and Marshall Langston, I dug a bit deeper, it is one reason I took so long getting here. One of the main purposes of constructing you people, rebuilding you was to give the Service agents who could perform those duties as you just completed without cause of concern and without inhibitions."

"Director," Langston spoke up. "I'm seeing the same interaction in this new group about to come out of the tanks that I saw with Cassi's group during the same time frame. Sir, they are being conditioned the same way, and we have six females in that group."

The Director rose from his chair and went to the door and spoke to his aide standing out in the hallway. Before he sat down, he spoke to Cassiopeia.

"My aide is going after Doctor Cooper. If there is any way possible to correct your conditioning, I promise, it will be done. And Marshall Langston, those people will not leave those tanks in the same condition. I don't care how much longer they need to be in there, or the expense, this will not be repeated."

"Thank you Director." Cassiopeia softly spoke.

Five hours later, Cassiopeia was ready to go back into a new tank, with untainted nanites. Doctor Cooper asked her before putting her under how she managed what she had done earlier.

"Doctor Cooper, one part of the programming in the nanite AI is the protection of its host. Tia, my AI, was not about to allow you to harm me, and once my body was in contact with the nanites in the tank, it or should I say I, released a large group of nanites into the tank by urinating, which was concealed since my legs were closed. Once those nanites were in the mist of virgin nanites, they spread like a virus, marking them as part of my protective system. From there all I had to do was tell Tia what I needed done."

"And your nanites removed the drugs from your system without them affecting you?"

"Yes. Doctor Cooper, I have great control over my body, but it is my mind you people messed with in a way that never should have happened. The Director has explained to me why it was done, but it was over done in my thinking. I'm eating a lot of guilt and pain because of what I have done to myself. Would I have done things differently if I had been a normal human being? I'd like to think I would have fulfilled my mission, just not in the same manner, and certainly not so eager to jump in bed with any man or woman willing to pay my price. That's the problem Doctor, I had no safe guards to tell me when to back away, when enough was enough."

"I'm sorry Cassiopeia. I never knew the extent the conditioning had on you or the others."

Two weeks later Cassiopeia exited the tank feeling refreshed and free of guilt even with the memories of what had transpired in the past. She knew she now had full control of her emotions and desires, plus Tia had been released from the blocks which prevented it from helping Cassiopeia in such a manner.

A week later Cassiopeia appeared in a sim with the new group of subjects and spoke to them about the changes they were feeling since their programing or conditioning had been changed and they were still unsure of what had happened to them since they no longer had the desires to copulate at any given time.

It was learned that the head programmer for that section of conditioning had taken the memorandum too literal, and added a few of their own perversions into the programming.

Cassiopeia would lecture the new group twice more before they left their tanks, and she escorted them to the training compound. This time dividers were provided between bunks to provide some measure of privacy, and the bunks were large enough for two people sharing it.

She told them it was only natural for two people to enjoy the closeness that sexual contact provides, but for them to understand they were not built for that and that alone, they had more serious things ahead of them.

Cassiopeia took the group out to a single grave. A grave for Simon Barnett and pointed out that he had been her lover, and that he was the first of their breed to die in service. Death traveled within the velocity of a bullet.

Mala and Jefferson went through the correction of their conditioning at the same time while the new group was still in their tanks. Cassiopeia waited until she delivered the new group to the training complex to ask Mala how it affected their love life. Mala told her it actually made it better since the desire was truly theirs, and not a condition they had to act on.

103

The new group had been in training for nearly a month when Gunther arrived, having been through the reconditioning after his long mission to the other side of the Union's universe, chasing a hacker who had stolen millions of credits from the Planetary Union's Exchequer.

The Marshalls service had built new quarters for the first group at the training complex, this time with individual apartments complete with sanitary facilities so they would have the privacy they were first denied. Cassiopeia and Gunther would spend hours in the common room talking about their adventures and lives out away from the group. It would be three weeks after his return that Cassiopeia took him to her bed, and would later agree with Mala that the sex was indeed better.

It would be over six months after Gunther returned that Robert returned from his time being repaired, and as with Gunther, it would take Cassiopeia weeks before she invited him to her room for the night. Sex between her and the two men was sporadic at best, and they went weeks without sleeping together.

Cassiopeia was finally at ease with her sexuality.

The Next Mission

After the debacle over the sexual programing, Langston was given full control over the Project as ten more subjects was introduced to the tanks. He brought Professor Smuthers fully back into the program as they monitored the progress of the new subjects.

Even though Robert was in top shape after his repairs, he was deemed psychologically unsuitable for high risk operations since watching Simon get killed in front of him, plus the trauma of his own wounds. He was assigned to the training complex to teach weapons, and only given very low risk assignments when another Marshall was not available.

Cassiopeia and Gunther took an assignment acting as a young, married couple. The Service had received reports of unusual activity from the crew of a transit freighter making the rounds between the frontier planets. Seven women reported they thought they had been raped during transit, but could not remember anything except how sore and bruised they were the next morning.

Those with mates could not remember anything of that night either, and two reported it happened twice during their transit. None of the females developed pregnancies due to this activity. It was noted that one couple never arrived at their destination, but the log of the freighter, listed as The Stewart, did not show the couple boarding even though they had purchased tickets.

Cassiopeia and Gunther traveled to the world, New Dawn by a Marshall's transport, then to Braylee, via a standard transporter. At Matthew's Landing on Braylee, they bought tickets to Cranston on the Stewart.

The documents they carried said they were from New Dawn and had Immigration Papers for Cranston. Cassiopeia's hair had grown out while at the Training Compound, and Gunther had let his hair grow plus a short beard. Both dress according to how someone from New Dawn of meager income would dress and carried only four pieces of luggage with them.

Two of the pieces of luggage looked like any normal, cheap cases someone from New Dawn might have purchased to carry their things in for transit. Both showed Customs seals from New Dawn and Braylee, meaning the ship's crew could not access them for inspection without breaking the seals. The other two had tags on them showing they had been inspected on both worlds, and they contained no hazardous materials or weapons.

The customs forms for the two sealed cases stated they contained heirlooms, and personal items when in fact, they carried their vests, weapons, and other items needed to fulfill their mission.

As they walked up the ramp to board the ship, Gunther stumbled, dropped his cases and fell into the First Officer who was at the top of the ramp to log their boarding. When Gunther grabbed the First Officer, he stuck a micro listening device to the First Officer's sleeve. Gunther apologized, handed over their boarding passes as Cassiopeia chided him for being so clumsy.

Gunther was traveling under the name of Sean Browning, while Cassiopeia was using Peggy Browning. Cassiopeia was dressed down and had let her hair look as if it had not seen a brush in several days. Gunther said she looked like a delicious mess.

In their assigned quarters, Gunther took out what appeared to be a cheap Pocket-Doc device which was fairly standard across the universe and accessed a special application which told them their quarters was bugged. They both instructed their AI's to tune in on the bug Gunther had planted as they put their things away while listening to the First Officer and others speaking. They finally heard what they were listening for.

The First Officer reported to the ship's Captain on the bridge and advised him the female who had boarded look like she would be enjoyable laid across a bed. The Captain said he got a decent look at her via the boarding ramp camera, and they would wait until they were two days out before enjoying her.

106

As soon as the Stewart was out of Braylee's gravity well, they were given a short tour of the ship. They were the only passengers for this transit, and except for the areas they were shown, they were restricted in moving around the ship. One place they were shown was the ship's kitchen and mess facilities. Gunther placed another bug in the mess, near where it was indicated the Captain sat during meals, and Cassiopeia placed one in the kitchen. Their AI's could easily monitor all the bugs, then let both of them know if something vital was mentioned by anyone in those premises.

There were eight total crew members on the ship counting the Captain and First Officer. Regulations for all ships in transit was a minimum of two personnel must be on the bridge at all times. This meant when the time came, they would have to deal with six individuals before moving to the bridge.

Just after what was considered the evening meal aboard the ship, Cassiopeia decided to give the crew something to listen too. She used her AI to talk to Gunther about it.

"Gunther, since they are listening, let's give them something to listen too."

"Alright how do you want to do it? Pretend you are blowing me, or us having sex."

Cassiopeia began taking her clothes off.

"Pretend hell, get busy and make a lot of noise."

They started with verbal foreplay which got the attention of the bridge crew who notified the Captain and First officer to come to the bridge. Luck favored them as the First Officer was still wearing his jacket with the bug on it as they were not allowed access to the bridge. The AI's were told to filter out their sounds and record only what came via the bugs for play back later.

Cassiopeia and Gunther took their time actually enjoying the moment while remembering to be louder than normal. Oral foreplay between them then down to actual business brought a variety of comments from the crew via the bugs.

107

Later as they relaxed from their exertions, they listened to the recordings from the bug. One comment that Cassiopeia smiled at was if she was good while drugged, they might have to try her fully conscious. It seemed the Captain liked screamers and Cassiopeia was very loud. But raping her while conscious meant they either spaced her later, or possibly sell her once tired of her. Either could explain the two missing females and their mates from the reports to the Marshalls Service.

The AI's basically kept watch during the night as they slept and the next, ship's day was just spent waiting for the shoe to drop. As it neared dinner time, they heard the Captain instruct the cook to prep the meal for their passengers so they could screw the female. Earlier in the day, both of them had taken soluble capsules packed with thousands of virgin nanites.

As soon as the nanites entered the system, the AI's brought them into their folds and stood by as they would be used to neutralize any drugs or poisons introduced during dinner. The other side of utilizing the nanites was they would analyze the substance, and the AI would advise the nature and effects of the substance so they could pretend to be affects by it.

Within thirty minutes after they had left the mess facility for their quarters, Cassiopeia was heard on the bridge complaining about not feeling well. Gunther commented he was feeling dizzy. Forty five minutes after dinner, the First Officer used his command access to open their compartment door to find Sean (Gunther) sprawled out in the room's chair, and Peggy (Cassiopeia) laid out half on the bed.

The First Officer and one of the mates picked Cassiopeia up and carried her to the Captain's cabin and laid her on his bed, then began to undress her. Tia was keeping Cassiopeia advised of location of each person in the room, as Gunther's AI, Clare, was advising him of Cassiopeia's situation, plus the one individual still in the room going through their personal things.

What no one noticed was a micro-spybot that was hovering just below the ceiling which was keyed to Tia, and followed

Cassiopeia as she was being carried away. Another one was keyed to Clare, and stayed with Gunther as he waited his time to strike.

The mate still in the room moved to Gunther to check his pockets and found himself flying across the room when Gunther hit him in the chest. Gunther moved quickly and insured the mate was out, then pulled a sealed case out and opened it. Disposable restraints were applied plus a gag to prevent him from yelling a warning in case he awoke too soon.

Gunther pulled his vest from the case and secured it before opening Cassiopeia's case and slinging her vest over his shoulder. With a Neural pistol in hand, he checked the passageway, before entering it, heading for Cassiopeia's location.

Cassiopeia listened to the remarks concerning her body and heard one comment that if they keep her, he was going to put his dick in her nice ass. She heard the Captain tell the man to be patient, then felt the bed move as she suspected the Captain was crawling up between her legs to mount her.

Gunther told Cassiopeia he was almost there which let her know she could act before she was penetrated by the Captain. He was about halfway up to her when she swung her legs out wide then wrapped them around his torso. She opened her eyes to see the surprise on the Captain's face.

"Surprise!" She quipped then broke four of his ribs as she crushed him with her legs. Cassiopeia then reached up with her left hand and held his head as she rapped him hard just behind his ear with her right fist, knocking him unconscious.

It only took seconds to disable the Captain in this manner, then she rolled over and pushed him off her, and the bed onto the deck. There were three other men in the room, all in various level of undress when she struck the nearest man in the throat, dropping him out of her way so she could execute a backward round house kick, catching that target in the ear with her heel.

As she was doing that, Gunther had came around the corner to the Captain's cabin and put a Neural dart in the cook, then a mate who had been standing in the corridor, waiting their turn. When Gunther stuck his head in the door, he saw Cassiopeia standing with her foot on the First Officer's neck.

"Honey, that is one hell of a view, but we still have to take the bridge."

Cassiopeia laughed then thumped the First Officer's head hard enough to render him unconscious. Gunther tossed her vest to her then moved towards the bridge. Cassiopeia quickly dressed, secured the unconscious men in the room, then in the passageway before going to join Gunther on the bridge.

When Cassiopeia joined Gunther, he had both men down and secured. Cassiopeia stepped past Gunther and hit the Emergency Beacon, then they drug both men back to the cargo bay, and placed them into the Custom's Isolation Cage.

They had no problem dragging the crew to the cage and Tia advised Cassiopeia how to change the code so they could secure the cage until a Marshall's transport could meet with them. The Emergency Beacon for this ship would notify the Marshall's transport that had been shadowing them to catch up and dock with them.

Back on the bridge, Gunther cut boost and fired the retros for thirty seconds, slowing the freighter down, then fired them again to cease all forward motion.

Cassiopeia went back to their quarters and checked the recorders in the cases to insure the spybots had recorded everything that had been done. She then took a sterile sample bag from the case and urinated in it, expunging the nanites which carried the drugs secreted in their dinner into it as further evidence against the ship's crew. She took another bag to Gunther who did the same.

Two hours later their comms on their vests notified them the Marshall's transport had them on their scope and would dock soon. After the transport docked with the Stewart, a prize crew came aboard to deal with the freighter, while a team came aboard to take charge of the prisoners. The only prisoner requiring medical treatment was the Captain due to the broke ribs cause by Cassiopeia.

Cassiopeia and Gunther went aboard the transport, to separate quarters as the prize crew continued on to Cranston with the supplies which had been paid for, especially the medical supplies. Any cargo that had additional travel beyond Cranston would be off loaded on Cranston, the transport fees paid to the Stewart would be returned to the consignee's once the Marshalls Service accessed the Stewart's accounts so they would not lose any credits, and still get their cargo which was paid for in advance.

It was a two month run back to Magnus for the Stewart's crew to stand trial for their crimes. The cook admitted during a video interview that one female and her mate had been spaced, while another female had been sold to a sex trafficker after being used for a couple of months after her mate had been spaced.

The prize crew discovered recordings of the rapes of several females, and recordings of the one that was sold servicing the men during various times before her being sold. She had been kept in one of the passenger quarters and used when any of the men wanted her.

By the time they arrived at Magnus, a Marine Assault team had assisted a Marshall in raiding the compound where the Stewart's Captain had sold the female on Hawthorne. That female was no longer there, but they rescued sixteen other females, some as young as twelve.

During the first two weeks aboard the Marshalls transport, Cassiopeia and Gunther stayed in their quarters, until she pulled him into hers one night after the evening meal. He stayed in those quarters with her for three weeks, even though several nights it was just sleeping together without any excitement.

Gunther did ask her one night as they lay in bed, just cuddling why she had not killed the Captain when she had him in a vulnerable position.

"Gunther, there was no need to kill him although I might have done him a favor in doing so, but then he would have gotten off lightly for his crimes."

"Yeah, if they give him the maximum, lobotomized, then a life of hard labor on Divergent."

"Even lobotomized, he'll know why he is there, working in that hellish place till either the labor or the heat takes what I didn't take from him. I hope he lives a long life."

Gunther never commented on her wish for a long life knowing how he would suffer on Divergent. Then there was the other prisoners who took advantage of the lobotomized prisoners in ways he didn't want to think about.

Before his correction, Gunther, like all the boys in the group had been bi-sexual without any thought about it, but since the conditioning had been corrected, he was straight heterosexual. But he remember the nights with Jefferson, or Robert, or Simon, often as a group, and the sex was kind, gentle in the taking and giving. But the hard cases on Divergent would not be gentle to those lobotomized. But even Gunther's pity only went so far, and he had to agree with Cassiopeia in that all of that crew lived long lives.

Once they had processed the prisoner's into the system on Magnus, presented their evidence before the Magistrate, they were free to do as they wished for the thirty days before the Stewart's crew went before a jury.

Cassiopeia returned to the Training Compound, packed her field pack and walked off into the plains surrounding the training site. She had to get her head together as she came to grips with the fact she had loved one man in her youth she could never have, and another that was buried at the Compound. Her time with Gunther was nothing more than trying to wash both from her heart without success.

She knew that if she stayed at the Compound she'd make a mistake with Gunther or possibly Robert, which would do none of them any good. She was finally free of the controls on her sexuality, but in removing those controls she found her true emotions were just as distracting, and even more painful.

Cassiopeia found it was easy to make love to Gunther that night to give the crew something to be eager for, and she felt no remorse for that, but the time spent with Gunther on the return trip was too good, too enjoyable, and too dangerous to pursue.

Mala had announced her intention of becoming pregnant which Cassiopeia though was wonderful for her. Mala's life with Jefferson was centered on the training site and they had the Director's assurances they would manage that site until their term of enlistment expired.

Cassiopeia queried Tia concerning a pregnancy considering the nanites in the body would attack a foreign substance. Tia assured her that if the AI was aware that the female wished to be pregnant, the nanites would actually help in that aspect, ensuring the sperm reached the egg to fertilize it. They could not predetermine the sex of the child, but once fertilized and beginning to develop could inform the host of the sex of the child they were carrying. The nanites would also ensure the child was healthy and brought to term.

She sat on a rise over thirty kilometers from the training site and just thought about her life. She would have never lived to see her twelfth birthday which made her laugh as she actually never really saw any of them with her partial blindness.

She was now facing the Law of Unintended Consequences by the fact she demanded her free will, which she actually did not have, but now that she had it, she was worried that she could not complete the bargain she had with the Marshalls Service in return for her current condition.

Cassiopeia had basically traded one mental prison for another.

With the aid Tia, Cassiopeia read the ancient Terran Bible, then studied Zen, Buddhism, and several other Terran religions, looking for a place she could reside. She read the modern All-Saints Bible and the Transformed Hindu Thesis. Cassiopeia left nothing untouched in her search for herself, and still came up empty.

On the eleventh day of her self-pilgrimage, Cassiopeia was recalled to the training site to confer with the trainees over a mission they had been given. Jefferson picked her up in the Complex's aircar to shorten her transit time back.

When she entered the classroom, thinking this would be another dry run like they had when her group graduated, Robert and Gunther were present, and she could tell by the looks on their faces without access their AI's this was no dry run.

She had hardly entered the room when Gunther keyed up the large monitor at the end of the room and the Director presented himself to the viewers.

"Lieutenant D'Auber, first of all, be advised you have been promoted to the rank of Captain in the Marshalls Service. Congratulations is all that can be extended for now as we have a lot to cover."

"Thank you Director. May I ask about my fellow teammates?"

"They have all been elevated one rank, but they already know that. Now here is what we have for you, and the group of trainees."

The world under discussion was Williamsburg, and the city was the planet capital also named Williamsburg. Young girls were disappearing off the streets and the local law enforcement officers could not seem to find out why, or where they had disappeared too.

A girl, age fourteen, was rescued from a bordello out on the southern rim on the frontier world of Plinkston, having disappeared nearly a year before while walking home from school.

The mission was simple. Find the source of disappearances and shut it down.

114

Cassiopeia was mission commander and her team consisted of the trainees. Robert and Gunther were logistical support only.

Moments later they received a massive data dump from Headquarters. Cassiopeia started barking orders.

"Alright people let's get everything organized, and spread out. Robert, I know these people are competent with their weapons, but go over every one of them. If you think a part might fail next year, replace it. Leave nothing to chance on this."

"Will do Cassi." As Robert headed for the barracks to begin his task.

"Gunther, there is no way eleven of us can just drop in on Williamsburg and say Hello, we need the Marshalls Service to come to the rescue. Get with Headquarters and begin setting up ID's, transit papers, everything we might need to go from here to there. We can always adjust that once we have a valid plan, and let them know and be ready to make the adjustments in a hurry."

"Got ya Cassi." Gunther went to the computer terminal in the classroom and began making the list.

Cassiopeia just let the students run with the task of getting the information sorted out and placed in some semblance of order. Her own thoughts about how to tackle this mission was disrupted by one of the students.

"Captain D'Auber…"

"Freeze, everyone freeze!" She commanded.

She looked around the room and saw she had everyone's attention.

"Pay close attention to what I am about to say. We will be going undercover and that means I am not Captain anything. Understand? You know who has been given command of this mission, and if all you do is refer to me as Captain every time I turn around, you just might make that mistake while undercover

115

and blow it wide open, placing not only myself at risk, but yourselves and others. So, just call me Cassi. Got that people?"

She let it sink in for a moment then turned to the person who had called out to her.

"Alright Bryan, what did you want?"

"Cassi, we have over a dozen missing persons reports over the past eight years. How do you want me to list them?"

"Simple Bryan, pull every piece of data from each report. Williamsburg is a city of over four million people, so if that person was at school then was heading home when they may have been kidnapped, locate the school, then the home and find the most logical route between the two and map it out, then take the next one and do the same on the same map until they are all done. Use different colors for each individual so if you have a possible variance in route, put that in with dashes. Got it?"

"Yeah, I was thinking it would be harder than that."

"Bryan, let me know when you get done if it was easy."

Two other people jumped in to assist Bryan as the others just took the statements and such from each case and looked for common grounds. Gunther came over to Cassiopeia, and leaned over to whisper to her.

"Cassi, Personnel has the request and are on it. The Director gave them a heads up, so they were prepared. Unless you need me, I'm going to take your gear to your quarters, then go see if Robert needs any help."

"Thanks Gunther. I've been fasting some while gone, but suddenly I'm starving."

"No problem Cassi, I'll take care of it."

Cassiopeia just stood back and let the trainees tackle the job of sorting through the data and arranging it into a decipherable form. She was noticing that the people were pairing up, male and

116

females, as if they had already been paring after hours. She had not noticed Mala entering the classroom until she spoke to her.

"Cassi, how's things going?"

"Oh, hi Mala. Sorry didn't see you come in. Is it me or do the folks at Headquarters have a disability when it comes to organizing data for an operation?"

Mala laughed a bit then responded.

"They are too compartmentalized and fight for their position in the pecking order. It can be a strain at times."

"That's for sure. I've noticed how the people are pairing up. Is this going to be a problem for me in the field?"

"No, and from what Gunther told me when I stopped by the barracks, this could work out for you." Mala commented.

"Cassi, a moment please." Came the call from across the room. Cassiopeia quickly identified the individual as Ruby. She was also a redhead and petite, even small than herself. Cassiopeia went over to Ruby.

"What do you need Ruby?"

"I was looking at the data you have Bryan working on, and only seven of the last twelve missing girls are from Williamsburg. Do we need to plot those also according to city?" Ruby asked.

"What do you think?" Cassiopeia put it back on her.

"Yes. Even if in a different location, it might tells us something, form a pattern that might not be noticed if left strictly to Williamsburg." Ruby responded after a moment's thought.

"Then what are you wanting for Ruby?" Cassiopeia asked with a smile.

Cassiopeia walked back to Mala.

"Mala, how's Ruby doing in the field training?" Cassiopeia asked.

"That girl is as dangerous as you ever were, maybe more so. Don't let her size fool you, she has banged up all of the boys in training, and one of them while in the rack." Mala laughed then continued. "She is quick, focused, and it seems due to her physical size, the programmers gave her an edge in strength, even if her body does not show it. If you are concerned about taking her into a hot situation, don't worry. If she's not the best shooter in the group, she is damn close to being it."

"That's good to hear, but then again Mala, we both know training and the real thing are totally separate beasts."

Mala never replied as they stood and watched the trainees working the data. They watched as the maps appearing on the large monitor began showing the routes and possible routes of the girls who had been kidnapped, but so far, only two had crossed.

Cassiopeia played a hunch and spoke to Tia.

**"Tia, I need a hack without the other end knowing they were violated."

**"Mistress, there are specific rules concerning hacks. If what you request falls within those rules, I can do what you need done." Tia responded.

**"Tia, I believe there is a possibility for suppression of evidence by one or more individuals within the Williamsburg Police Department. My concern is, if I ask for specific information through normal channels, either the information I ask for will be tampered with, or the people we are looking for will be alerted to our investigation and go to ground."

**"Mistress, I have logged your words and if required will transmit them to the Marshalls Service Legal Department, but be aware before I attempt to gather the information you will next ask for, that you may have to defend your actions before a Board of Inquiry."

**"I am aware of such circumstances Tia. Please log my acknowledgement of your warning and prepare to do as I ask."

**"It is so logged Mistress. What information do you need?"

**"I need you to access the files for juvenile or youth gang activities in the stricken areas. All files which might provide my team with information concerning dates and times of activities especially in relationship to the kidnappings."

**"Yes Mistress."

Gunther showed up a few minutes later with a bowl of vegetable soup with large chunks of beef in it, along with a bottle of her favorite fruit drink. She took it to one of the vacant tables and sat down and tried to relax and eat.

Cassiopeia ate her fill, then pushed the bowl away and just watched the trainees work the problems. She had to smile in that as serious they were in tackling the problem, they joked and tried to have a bit of fun while working. It dawned on her that the working pairs seemed to know what their partner wanted or needed without speaking and that had to be via their AI's as she had taught them in the first week of training. This kept the noise level down in the classroom.

**"Mistress, this is taking longer that projected to comply with your request."

**"I understand Tia. I didn't expect an immediate answer to the problem."

Cassiopeia knew that time and distance played into finding and developing the information she had asked for, so there was no need to be impatient.

"Cassi, the routes are plotted based upon the parents statements and the possible alternate routes based upon the locations being traveled to and from. But except for two intersecting, I don't see a pattern here." Bryan advised Cassiopeia.

"Bryan, you are looking at a one dimensional view of a street map, but what is missing from that map?" She asked him.

119

He stood for several minutes looking at the map then chuckled.

"Buildings, especially any stores or shops the girls might stop to check out clothes, or any manner of items." He replied.

"Well?" She put to him.

Bryan went to the computer and posted an inquiry concerning the physical terrain for the map, buildings, and possible side streets not normally listed. He added a request for specific locations along the plotted routes of various stores, asking the girls on the team their advice on what to ask for. Slowly the map was filled in with the data he had requested.

One aspect of the physical map was that the location where the two routes intersected was a candy store on a street corner. They didn't know if the candy store might have anything to do with the kidnappings, but it was recommended they look into the background of the store owner which Cassiopeia approved.

She shut them down at 2200 hours to rest, telling them they'd pick it up in the morning after breakfast. Tia was still active in her search of police records, but this did not bother Cassiopeia as she retired to her own quarters, unpacked her things, put what needed to be cleaned in the refresher, took a shower and laid down. Sleep came quickly.

Tia woke her at her regular time of 0500 in the morning. Cassiopeia fixed an energy drink, dressed, then went to the classroom. Tia had advised her she had finished the program concerning the gangs and was ready to post it when instructed. Cassiopeia asked her when she finished it, with Tia responding 0317 hours, but felt the Mistress needed her rest, and the information would still be available once the day started. Cassiopeia thanked her for the courtesy knowing that arguing with Tia was a waste of time.

Once the team was gathered in the classroom, Cassiopeia had Tia post the gang information to the route map.

"People, take notice of what has been posted. In Williamsburg, a juvenile youth gang has been operating for nearly two decades, recruiting new members as the older ones moved on to other things. Within the time frames the girls came missing, the gang caused a disruption within four city blocks of the possible routes the girls were taking causing the local law enforcement personnel to converge on that location, and away from where the girls have disappeared."

She moved to the large monitor and caused the smaller map of the town of Hardinge to expand.

"Here we have the same situation with another gang known to be associated with the one in Williamsburg. We can find this at each city girls have been kidnapped."

Cassiopeia reduced Hardinge, returning Williamsburg to the full size then turned to the team.

"First of all, no where in the reports is mentioned of any possible connection with these gangs and the missing girls. I suspect someone in the local police departments are purposely leaving out that information as requested by the Marshalls Service."

"Dirty cops?" Lukas proposed.

"Yes Lukas, that is a very real possibility. Let us suppose that we have one or more former gang members who had never been arrested, becoming law enforcement officers. As long as the gangs visible crimes are minor, misdemeanors, local law enforcement will only consider them a nuisance. Each one of the activities the day the girls came up missing, the gangs only was classified as disturbing the peace with no property damage. In each case, local law just broke up the gathering, then went about their business."

She paused to let them consider what she had told them.

"One last thing here. According to what reports there are available, there are four possible locations from which the Williamsburg gang operates from. Missing girls could be held at

121

any of them, but which one is undetermined. How do we deal with this without involving the local police? Go to work people."

Cassiopeia liked what she saw as the group gathered chairs into a circle and went to work exchanging ideas on how to deal with this situation instead of pairing up to submit a list of ideas.

**"Tia, send a memo, Eyes Only, to the Director advising him what I have done concerning the hacking of Williamsburg Law Enforcement Agencies, and what we might have discovered."

**"Yes Mistress."

Cassiopeia took a seat away from the team so they could work out the problem of locating the place where girls might be held by the gang if they were the kidnappers.

Gunther and Robert came in and watched the team, then her for a moment, then pulled up chairs on both sides of her and sat down. They had hardly been seated when Gunther reached over and took Cassiopeia's left hand in his, then Robert took her right hand. She looked at one then the other with a puzzled look on her face.

"Cassi, you were about to wear the flesh off your fingers rubbing your hands they way you were doing." Robert spoke.

"Yeah, doll, everything about you looks calm, except for the way you were worrying your hands." Gunther pitched in.

Cassiopeia looked at the part of her left hand she could see in Gunther's to see that it was red from being rubbed. Looking at her right hand, it had the same look. She slowly pulled her hands back from them and laid them in her lap.

"Thank you gentlemen, but we do not wish to give the trainees the idea that I just let anyone hold my hands."

Both men chuckled knowing how she preferred for a man to hold her.

"What have you got Cassi?" Gunther asked.

She gave them a short, but in depth briefing of what Tia had discovered, and what the trainees, the team was currently doing.

"Have you got a plan?" Robert asked her.

"I have a dozen plans, all worthless at the moment." She replied. "Robert, how do their weapons look?"

"They're in great shape. They've taken good care of them." Robert replied to her question.

**"Mistress, we have a reply from the Director. He acknowledges the requirement to hack Williamsburg and has signed off on the requirement. He says to proceed as needed and with caution"

**"Thank you Tia."

The debate amongst the team went on for hours as they tried to develop a plan. Mala had came over for a time and gathered up Robert and Gunther, then went to the barrack's kitchen to prepare a buffet style meal for the team so they would not have to stop working.

Cassiopeia was mildly surprised that the team could sit for hours debating one plan after another without seeming to break the calm of the discussion, but just over an hour after the midday meal, in which they continued to discuss plans, the debate got heated.

As the voices got louder, Cassiopeia noticed the calmest voice belonged to Ruby, and it seemed everyone was directing their protests to her.

Ruby finally stood and stepped over in front of the boy called Franklin, and this time Cassiopeia plainly heard her words.

"Franklin, I know how you feel about me, but you also know I can take care of myself. We've been debating this for hours without a single good plan or option to exploit. This idea gives us one."

Ruby then stepped between Franklin and Lukas as she started towards Cassiopeia with the others jumping up and following.

Even before Ruby could speak, it seemed everyone was trying to get a word in against Ruby's idea until Ruby told them to shut up.

"Captain D'Auber, Cassiopeia, I have an idea which as you can tell the others hate, but please, hear me out."

Cassiopeia looked at Ruby then around at the others before speaking.

"Alright, everyone hold their comments until asked for. Ruby you have the floor."

"Thank you. No matter how we squeeze it, we cannot be sure which location the gang is using as their headquarters or where if any girls are being held. We don't have enough strength to hit all four locations at once and if a single one of them is a false front, then we have created an incident with the locals."

"Granted." Cassiopeia responded.

"So, the only way, the surest way to locate and secure the right place is for someone to be inside to begin with. Now from what we have seen, the gang recruits off the street, and they recruit young. None of my male team members could qualify for such plus the time it would take for them to get deep inside the gang and locate the correct location, several more girls could go missing."

"What are you proposing Ruby?" Cassiopeia asked thinking she already knew the answer.

"Let them kidnap me. With my size and looks I can pass for someone fourteen, and maybe if I change my clothes, even my basic appearance, even younger."

"Ruby, that is a high risk situation for you." Cassiopeia responded.

"Cassiopeia. Several things I have considered that has not been brought up in discussion. One, how are they taking these girls without causing a disturbance? Two, how are they transporting them from the kidnap site to where ever they are holding them? Three, how are they getting them off planet? We need to get inside of them as fast as possible, and if you, or anyone else can think of a better way, I'm all for it."

"Gunther, you ready to get back into the field?" She spoke to Gunther as she was looking at Ruby.

"What's on your mind Cassi?"

"We go as Ruby's parents to cover her being in school and such."

"Cassi I hate to point this out, but we are not that much older than Ruby would be in this operation."

"It takes a little doing, but our AI's can modify our looks, not change them, but modify them. I learned this doing my prostitute thing while looking for Xeno Fillage. We can age ten years, and that should cover us well enough."

The looks on the faces of the team when Cassiopeia mentioned working as a prostitute showed they were not aware of her past assignments. She would later explain to Gunther that while working in the bordello, her entire body was covered with tattoos, from her ankles to her neck, down to her wrists, all supplied by the nanites, then later removed as they chased Xeno to Tantus.

"Alright Ruby, you're the target. Everyone else pair up so Gunther can arrange new papers for everyone. Gunther, we all can't drop on the planet at the same time from the same location. We need to get as much of the team in Williamsburg as possible before we place Ruby on the ground, and at risk."

Gunther never commented as he left his seat and went to work. Ruby just smiled at Cassiopeia, then left with the team following as they first cleaned up after the mess created from the

125

buffet, then packaged all of the data provided so it could be stored away.

Cassiopeia sat for a long time thinking Ruby was right, her idea would put them in contact quicker than anything else they had came up with. And they all had to face the reality that as Marshalls, they were to place their own lives and well-being second to that of the people they were sworn to protect.

That evening the first two pairs left for Williamsburg with their first stop at the Marshalls Service Logistic Center to be clothed and outfitted for the mission. Theirs would be the longest route to Williamsburg.

Cassiopeia called Ruby over to talk to her in the privacy of her own room.

"Ruby, you heard my comment about working as a prostitute during an assignment. Now let me explain a couple of things to you. Yes, I had sex with dozens of men and a few women during that time working in a bordello looking for Xeno Fillage. It was during that time I found it was too easy to allow a man to use me however they desired and to be honest, I enjoyed being used. It was during that time I felt something was not right with our conditioning, our programming."

"What does this have to do with this mission?" Ruby asked.

"Do you remember the first days and nights in the sims? How sex was seemingly a necessity?"

"Yes Cassi, I do. By the end of the first week I had taken Frank and Justin to my bed." Ruby responded.

"By the end of the first month, we had an orgy in the sims. Mala and I took on the boys all at once. I took three of them at one time and never looked back. Our first night here in the barracks, we did it again, this time real flesh on flesh. Ruby, this was wrong. That first orgy I was in reality only twelve years old even though the sims said I was much older. But this is bringing me to my point."

126

Cassiopeia paused.

"When I returned after completing the mission to bring Xeno Fillage to justice, which a Liger handled that for me, I rebelled against the system, against the Psych Docs and my conditioning. We were all programmed, male and females to engage in sex for no other reason than to do it. It was discovered the programmer took their instructions too literal and then some by putting a few of their own perversions into the mix."

She paused again.

"Remember the last month you were in the sims, and I came to lecture all of you concerning sexual activity, and how the urges to copulate with another had faded? That was the reconditioning that took place in you and the others as I had also undergone reconditioning to make me more normal in that aspect."

"Yes Cassi, I remember your lectures, again, what does this have to do with the mission?"

"I'm concerned that you may be raped before we can get to you."

"Cassi do you think that I haven't considered that also? For one, they will not be getting a virgin so they are not stealing anything from me, second, depending on how soon you can affect a rescue, I may have to let one or two of them use me to keep them distracted. But if we can shut their operation down, even rescue a few girls, then it will just have to be what it is."

"Ruby, rape is an act of violence. An act to render the victim unable to control what is happening to them, at that time and possibly in the future."

Ruby chuckled.

"If one is on top of me when you bust in, he will not come off me breathing unless they have me chained to the bed."

"Alright then Ruby, I felt I had to say what I have said, now go get some rest and get ready for transit. We leave tomorrow night."

"Thanks for your concern Cassi. Now don't call, I'll call you because Frankie leaves in the morning and I intend to wear him out tonight."

"Franklin?"

"Yes." She said as she stood up. "Didn't you have a favorite?"

"Yes I did Ruby, and he's lying under a slab of cold marble across the way."

Ruby's smile turned neutral as she just nodded her head and left Cassiopeia alone with her thoughts.

Later that night as her head lay on Robert's stomach he brought up the mission.

"Cassi, why are you taking Gunther instead of me on this mission?"

"Robert, you are going as backup logistics. You're going as a Marshall assigned to Williamsburg."

"That's not what I meant and you know it."

"Have the Psych Docs released you back to full duty yet?"

"No, and you already know that."

"Robert, I have already lost Simon, I'm not going to risk losing you because you freeze up or fold. This discussion is closed."

Robert hated what she had said, but also she had just told him she held him closer to her heart than she did Gunther. They made love one more time before he had to leave ahead of her for Williamsburg.

She lay alone in her bed thinking Robert had bought the lie as neither men meant more than temporary comfort to her.

Williamsburg

The entire team had been on the ground three weeks when they were alerted that one of the possible transport freighters that took the kidnapped girls off world was due to land at the Williamsburg Space Port. Two more girls had been taken from other locations, and each day Ruby walked to and from school, taking the same path that intersected the candy store.

There was not much information of the owner of the candy store other than he had been in business for over thirty years, and there was no known record of his causing trouble. He lived above the candy store with his wife and his two sons had grown and left Williamsburg.

As the landing of the freighter came closer, Ruby reported she was being watched by a different boy each day that they could identify as being part of the gang working that area. Ruby also noticed that there were certain boys at school everyone avoid when possible.

Ruby was a block from reaching the candy store when the call went out to law enforcement of a disturbance four blocks west of the store. This put the team in motion, moving to locations they could respond from to assist Ruby if they went after her.

Ruby's AI, Mags, was broadcasting their location every two minutes allowing the team to keep track of her. Just as Ruby passed the candy store the owner called out to her.

"Hey girl, come here a minute."

As she stepped to face him, he pointed a Neural Dart pistol at her and fired. Ruby went down as predicted, but Mags was unharmed by the electric shock since it was insolated from such weapons and EMP. But Ruby was not knocked out as her nanites absorbed the electric shock and she just went into an acting mode for the players.

*"This is Ruby, the candy store owner just shot me with a Neural Dart and is dragging me into the store." She broadcast through her AI.

The team was moving, watching for gang members who might be watching the exterior of the store. Justin and Peggy took out two members hiding in an alley before they could bring their communicator up to issue a warning. They quickly secured them then moved to the back of the candy store.

*"I'm being taken down steps in the back of the store by the owner and another person."

This gave everyone a more precise location as each team member had been in the store once and knew there was a door at the rear of the store.

*"I'm being placed on a bed and they are taking my clothes off me. Any time people."

At that point, anything she could hear was transmitted to the rest of the team.

"Damn Joseph, I'm going to enjoy busting this one. Wake her up so she can scream when I shove my cock in her."

"Yeah Dad, but don't ruin her, I want to enjoy that pussy too."

"Hell boy, take her ass cause my cock is going to rip her wide open."

*"Gang, I hear whimpering off to my left."

At that point the team converged on the store with Justin and Peggy covering the rear. Cassiopeia was the first into the store and rushed to the back door. Opening it, there was the stairway up to the apartment, and the stairs leading down into the basement.

Cassiopeia motioned for Franklin and Suzette to take the apartment as she carefully opened the basement door and started down with Max behind her with the rest of the team and Gunther bringing up the rear as planned.

Just as the one called Joseph was about to stick Ruby with a stimulant, she opened her eyes, grabbed him by the arm and tossed him over the small bed she was on, hitting the near wall head on.

The old man had his pants down and was masturbating to get himself erect as Cassiopeia entered the room, and shot him in the ass with a Neural dart.

Ruby was off the bed and grabbing her clothes as Cassiopeia passed her, handing her a spare Neural pistol. Cassiopeia's goal was not the caged girls lining one wall of the basement, but another door at the back of the room.

Opening the door Cassiopeia discovered two things. First it was a tunnel, and the second there was a group of gang members in it coming to the door. Cassiopeia fired twice, taking out the first two gang members, but one of those behind those two had a short, barreled shotgun and fired.

Cassiopeia was hit in the neck and face by the first blast of the shotgun, then in her left side as she was going down by the second blast. Her protective skull cap protected her brain, but she was seriously wounded before Max, who was still following her dropped the individual with the shotgun, and exchanged fire with another who had a pistol, but never scored on Max.

**"Stay with me Mistress, let's give the nanites a chance to work."

**"Let me go Tia, let me die."

**"I cannot Cassiopeia, it is my responsibility to take care of you. Stay with me, help me take care of you."

**"Why can't I feel anything?"

**"It's because I shut off your nerve receptors. Gunther is coming to be with you and he has an emergency injection of additional nanites so I can stop the bleeding and reroute your blood supply to your brain."

**"Let me die Tia, I'm so tired of this life."

**"Gunther is injecting you now. No Mistress, I have no choice, no option here but to do everything possible to keep you alive. Now go to sleep as I am going to shut you down and let you rest."

Events moved quickly as Robert, who had been monitoring the communications between the team members notified the Marshalls Transport which had been lying off Williamsburg's third moon to come in and get Cassiopeia so they could put her in their Med-Deck's tank.

Robert then ordered an ambulance sent to the candy store as he also notified the local police of the Marshall's actions at that store. He also ordered the police to pick up every member of the local gang under his authority.

Gunther picked Cassiopeia up and carried her upstairs where Suzette met them with the store owners wife in custody. Franklin was still upstairs, going through anything which might hold papers, evidence against the store owners. He found a note giving him time and date of the transport arriving telling him they were the ones moving the kidnapped girls off planet to be sold as prostitutes.

Suzette pushed the wife down onto the floor and told her if she moved she would regret it, then went to work on Cassiopeia's wounds, bandaging her face to keep dirt from the wounds, then starting a fluid replaced process in both arms.

It took Gunther's Marshalls identification to prevent the ambulance from taking Cassiopeia to the nearest hospital instead of the Space Port to meet with the transport that was less than an hour out, and had called for a priority landing ahead of any other incoming ships.

Franklin notified the transport of the note concerning the incoming freighter. From there the transport notified the Fleet, and every Fleet ship within the sector converged to intercept the freighter.

133

**"Gunther, she lives, yet she wishes to die. I've done all I can do here; the rest is up to the Saints and hopefully a tank can keep her with us."

**"Thank you Tia."

Gunther stayed with Cassiopeia until she was lowered in the tank aboard the transport. Once in the tank, the transport just stayed in place until the team and their prisoners could be boarded.

In the basement were cages containing five girls who had been kidnapped and repeatedly raped in preparation for their being sold. Two of the girls were from other cities and had been raped before being brought to Williamsburg. Ruby was able to talk to them once they calmed down, knowing they had been rescued from their situation. Both stated it was the youth gangs that had kidnapped and raped them.

Orders were sent out to arrest the gang members from the other cities, along with the gangs in the cities that had other girls missing, but location unknown at this time.

A Fleet Fast Destroyer caught the freighter as it entered the Williamsburg solar system and boarded it. They were warned by the Captain of the Destroyer, that if they were transporting kidnapped females, and any harm came to those females, he, as a Fleet Captain could hold court on them, and have them spaced as punishment.

The Marines who boarded the freighter found three girls locked in a single room with bare essentials, and all showed signs of being used by members of the crew. The freighters crew was secured and a prize crew placed on the freighter to insure it landed safely on Williamsburg.

Robert spent two months overseeing the investigation on Williamsburg as gang members were rounded up, and dirty cops were identified by records found in the candy store. The freighter provided information where eight females had been sold into prostitution on other planets.

Marshalls converged on those worlds and were able to recover five of the eight. Two of the girls had died while in prostitution, and one had been sold to another freighter Captain who they later learned had kept the girl to service his crew. She was later recovered along with two small children from her contact with the crew.

The Marshalls Service brought in a team of Psych Docs to help the raped girls move back into society along with their parents who had to deal with young girls who had been traumatized by their rape.

Gunther never left the side of Cassiopeia's tank as they sat on the ground at Williamsburg, watching her vital signs. He tried several ties to contact Tia, but without success. The tanks computer monitor showed Tia to be active telling Gunther she just refused to talk with him as she was focused on repairing Cassiopeia.

Another Marshalls transport arrived to help with the prisoner load as every gang member was removed from the planet in a very public way. Eighteen law enforcement officers were also removed from the planet, and five more were charged locally for crimes associated with the gangs, but not involved in the kidnapping.

It would take months in the courts on Magnus before the case was closed.

Cassiopeia was transferred from the transports tank to one of the special tanks at the Project Complex on Magnus.

The Return

Cassiopeia slowly woke inside the tank at the Project Complex and began to cry. She recognized she was in a sim once again, and that she was still alive.

"Stop your crying young lady."

Cassiopeia looked around and found Thomas Langston standing in a corner watching her as she lay on a hospital bed in the sim.

"What are you doing here?"

"I'm here because you need me here. Cassi, you fought Tia for months trying to die when she was working so hard to keep you alive."

"What have I to live for Thomas? Tell me, what?"

"Love Cassi, you are loved."

"Who could love me?"

"That's for you to discover Cassi, but if Lauren and I did not have such a good life, I would forget our age difference and try to make you a very happy young lady."

"You're just saying that to get me to keep fighting."

"Then keep fighting and find out who else loves you. I have to go now, but I will be checking on you daily. If you wish to talk, let me know."

Langston disappeared from the sim leaving Cassiopeia alone in her hospital room.

**"Tia, are you there?"

Her bed elevated her head more, then a miniature version of herself appeared in front of her as if standing on the bed.

**"Yes Cassiopeia, I'm here."

**"Is that what you look like Tia?"

**"I am your AI, and you gave me a feminine name. Now what can I do for you?"

**"Was Thomas Langston lying to me about being loved?"

**"No Mistress, he was not."

**"Who was Thomas talking about?"

**"No Mistress, I agree with Master Thomas. Get well and find out for yourself. According to studies, the discovery of such is more satisfying if you discover it for yourself."

**"But you are supposed to respond to my questions, give me the answers I need to fulfill my function."

**"And Mistress Cassiopeia, you begged me to let you die against my basic programming which would have also killed me. No Mistress, this time I refuse to assist you since this is a personal situation, not a Marshalls Service requirement."

Cassiopeia sat for what she considered a long time before speaking again.

**"How long have I been in treatment?"

**"Fourteen months counting the time Master Gunther got you to the tank in the transport right after you were wounded."

**"Anyone else injured in the raid?"

**"No Mistress, only you."

**"Thank you Tia, put me back to sleep and don't bother me unless you determine it is important."

**"As you wish."

Cassiopeia awoke but this time she recognized this was a real hospital room and not a sim.

**"Tia, how long was I out?"

**"Seventeen months total Mistress."

**"Thank you."

Cassiopeia went back to sleep knowing her future was still being written, and hoped she had some control over it before it was done. When she next awoke, she was not alone in her room.

"Robert, what are you doing here?"

"Gee thanks Cassi. No glad to see you, no how are you, just a what are you doing here?"

"I'm sorry Robert. How are you doing?"

"Good, the Docs have returned me to full duty and I'm leaving soon for Winchester to take over the office there as the Senior Federal Marshall."

"Federal Marshall?"

"Oh, that's right. While you were out, the Parliament voted to change the Unions title to just the Federation of Planets, which now makes us Federal Marshalls. Look, I just stopped by to say goodbye."

"Robert, what about us if you are gone?"

"Cassi let's be honest here. I was just passing the time for you and we both know it. You lied to me before Williamsburg to ease the fact I wasn't to be involved in the raid. But don't worry about me. I found a companion in Suzette, and she is going with me to Winchester."

"Good for you Robert. I wish you many years of happiness."

Robert moved to her and gave her a quick kiss. Then started to leave. At the door he stopped and turned back to her.

"Gunther physically carried you to the transport's tank, then sat by your tank ever day that you were on the transport. He only left it to eat, clean himself, or when the medics asked him to leave as they tended to your tank. He even slept by it. Colonel

Langston had to order him to the barracks once you were placed in the tanks here at the Project. Cassi, the time is now and he is waiting for you. If you pass him by, then all of this was a waste of time. Anyway, if you are ever in the Winchester area, stop by and say hello."

With that he left, closing the door behind him leaving her to consider what he had said about Gunther.

Cassiopeia spent two more weeks in the hospital undergoing the required Psych exams, and physical exams from being wounded.

Mala and Jefferson stopped by once to show her their son, who they had named Simon. Neither spoke of Gunther, and she never asked about him.

Gunther watched as the aircar landed in front of the barracks, but only one person got out of it before it lifted and turned back towards the capital. The person's long red hair fluttered in the light breeze as she walked to the grave across the way from the barracks.

He watched the familiar walk, the shift of her hips as she moved with precise steps to the grave. Gunther could not stop himself from going to her as he watched her kneel at the grave. At first he could not tell what she was doing as it seemed her hands were moving around the cold marble slab with covered Simon's grave.

Gunther stopped about a meter back from Cassiopeia and just waited as he watched her pull weeds from around the marble that she could reach kneeled down. She spoke first.

"Gunther, I just came here to say goodbye to Simon, and let him know that unless you have changed your feelings for me, I'm going to let you woo me, and do me all the way to the altar."

"Why would I do that Cassi?"

She stood and turned to him.

"Because you actually love me for me. Am I wrong?"

"No Cassi, but I never knew how you really felt about me."

She walked over and kissed him. When they separated, they didn't speak as he picked up her bag and they walked to her quarters. It wasn't until they were laying in bed, recovering from what Cassiopeia was the best sex of her life because it wasn't sex, it was making love as only lovers could do it.

Cassiopeia and Gunther spent their honeymoon on a Marshalls Fast Transport on the way to Pandora to investigate the possible embezzlement of Federation Funds by the Settler's Office on Pandora. They closed the case in three months before they were ordered to Germanica to investigate the death of the head of their government.

But those are stories for another time.

About The Author

Leon Michaels is the author of several novels and short stories that reflect his twenty-three years of military service. Michaels enlisted in the Marine Corps in 1970 and has memberships in the Veterans of Foreign Wars, the American Legion, the Disabled American Veterans organizations, NRA, and Rotary International. In 1971, he married his high school sweetheart, raised three daughters and has three grandsons. He calls Creek County, Oklahoma home.